Praise for Lauren Dane's
Beneath the Skin

"There were some hot, alphas in the story that are just screaming my name now. I will be revisiting them! Overall *Beneath the Skin* was a good book with some yummy characters!"

~ *Fiction Vixen*

"I love *Beneath the Skin*!! The de la Vega Cat series is one of my favorites and definitely a reread. I hope there is another story in the works."

~ *Guilty Pleasures Book Reviews*

"Packed full of steamy love scenes, old grudges, betrayal, and witty banter between the characters, *Beneath the Skin* is a great story about were-cats standing up for their people and finding love in the middle of war."

~ *Limecello*

"I am a huge fan of Lauren Dane and *Beneath the Skin* is yet another fantastic read of hers. Gibson is pure alpha and he way he is described oozes sexuality..."

~ *Sensual Reads*

Look for these titles by
Lauren Dane

Now Available:

Reading Between The Lines
To Do List
Sweet Charity
Always

de La Vega Cats
Trinity
Revelation
Beneath the Skin

Chase Brothers
Giving Chase
Taking Chase
Chased
Making Chase

Petal, Georgia
Once and Again

Visits to Petal
Alone Time

Cascadia Wolves
Wolf Unbound
Standoff
Fated

Print Anthologies
Holiday Seduction
Holiday Heat

Beneath the Skin

Lauren Dane

SAMHAIN PUBLISHING

Samhain Publishing, Ltd.
11821 Mason Montgomery Road, 4B
Cincinnati, OH 45249
www.samhainpublishing.com

Beneath the Skin
Copyright © 2013 by Lauren Dane
Print ISBN: 978-1-60928-933-1
Digital ISBN: 978-1-61921-052-3

Editing by Anne Scott
Cover by Angela Waters

First Samhain Publishing, Ltd. electronic publication: April 2012
First Samhain Publishing, Ltd. print publication: January 2013

Dedication

To my readers who enable me to keep on writing this family—thank you for all your support!

Thanks always go to my husband for being so supportive and loving. I don't think I could get even half as much done if you weren't there to deal with the kids and all other stuff when I hit deadlines.

My editor, Anne Scott, who I am so fortunate to be able to work with, is awesome. Thank you for all the incredibly hard work and awesome edits.

Chapter One

Gibson de La Vega didn't think much of the Bringer he sat across the table from. And he didn't like having his time wasted with petty dominance games either.

Cats lived by a set of clear-cut rules. You didn't enter anyone else's territory without permission and you sure as hell didn't go bringing in, what was to some, nearly an entire jamboree's worth of cats.

And yet, this was exactly the scenario he was faced with.

Ten cats showed up in de La Vega territory without prior notice from a jamboree they had very little knowledge of, much less a relationship with.

It wasn't that he didn't enjoy the occasional spanking of an out-of-line feline. He nearly smiled at that. But these were clearly inferior cats who knew they had no leg to stand on with this bullshit. It would be easy enough to make them submit, but it was the principle of the thing.

Their actions made no sense. Which either rendered them witless or they had an ulterior motive. He didn't like either scenario. Sometimes dumb was more dangerous than calculated.

"You come into our territory bringing *ten* cats without obtaining permission. This makes me wonder why. And I try to contact your Alpha and he's suddenly not available? Not very professional of him, I must say." He sipped the thick, dark Cuban coffee but didn't miss the scent of fear sweating through the pores of the human lawyer the cat had brought with him.

Another slap. To have brought a human to a meeting of shifters was the worst sort of insult. Worse than bringing that many jaguars without even a head's up.

"Gibson, we don't recognize the authority of your family. We can travel anywhere we like without your permission." The human sat back, hands folded like Gibson gave a fuck what he thought. As if Gibson hadn't just sent his people to gather these stupid fucks up like wayward children and brought them before him. They already *were* recognizing his authority.

He let his gaze slide over the human, ignoring him for the moment. Gibson came from a family of lawyers, so it wasn't like he was impressed by a few letters behind a guy's name or anything.

He showed his teeth and let his cat rise enough to fill his eyes. The Bringer started and quickly averted his gaze.

"Did you think we wouldn't notice? You come into our territory with ten cats. What kind of team do you run that you wouldn't take offense to such a thing? And that you seemingly wouldn't notice. Sloppy. You will be gone in an hour." He drained his cup and stood. "When you've cleared the city limits you may call my office and start the process again. Correctly this time."

"Gibson, we've already made clear—"

He narrowed his gaze and focused on the human again. "Let me be *clear* with you so there are no further little misunderstandings. My friends and family call me Gibson. You are neither. Second, I couldn't care less what humans think about our laws. They're not for you. This is de La Vega territory. I am the Bringer, the only authority that counts here is mine.

Now take your pet with you and get the hell out of here before I show you what a real jaguar acts like."

With that, he turned and walked out, giving them an example of a real slap in the face, shifter style, by giving them his back. They were nothing to him. Even a room of them held no threat.

Waiting just around the corner was Dario, his second in command. Gibson filled him in on the meeting. "I want them to be escorted. And I want them to know it. If they don't get the fuck out right quick then I want them tossed out."

Dario would do it the way Gibson wanted. Which was why Gibson had promoted him to second after his brother-in-law Saul had taken some sabbatical to be with his wife in Europe where she'd landed a job. It was good to give orders people understood. That way there was no room for misinterpretation. He wasn't pleased by misinterpretation.

"On it. I'll update you on progress." Dario waited for Gibson's nod to free him and then headed out.

Less than an hour later, Gibson stalked down the long corridor toward his oldest brother's office. Max de La Vega wasn't only the oldest, he was now the Alpha of the jamboree, having taken over from their father just months before.

"You aren't bloody." Max raised a brow as Gibson entered. "I take it they showed you their belly?"

Gibson snorted and tossed himself into a chair. "They brought a human lawyer with them. Told me they don't recognize our authority and would travel when and where they liked."

The hair on Gibson's arms rose as Max's cat sounded in his rather feral growl. "They did not."

Gibson laughed then. Leave it to his brother to be as upset by the lawyer part as the slap in the face by the other cats. "They did. Called me Gibson. Twice."

"And you resisted ripping his head off and beating the other with his spine? Clearly you're mellowing in your old age."

"None of them is worth the effort. I told them to get the fuck off our land. Gave them an hour. Put three men on it." He glanced at his watch. "Time's nearly up. My men called already, they're complying apparently. If they don't, we'll toss them out physically."

"I'll await the call from their alpha."

"If he can be found. I've had some difficulty with that."

"If he knows what's good for him he'll materialize and do it soon. Can't imagine what he's thinking. Ten? That's a hell of a lot of cats to bring into another territory. Especially without permission. Is he trying to provoke an incident? Or just stupid?"

Gibson had been thinking this over since he'd met them face to face. "I'm trying to work that out myself. Their Bringer averted his eyes and showed proper respect. But he didn't say more than five words. He wasn't in charge of the situation.

"So it could be they've got a Bringer who is weak, plain and simple. They're a small enough jamboree that their population just doesn't have a stronger cat. I've never met Bertram, the Alpha, so I don't know what he's like."

It was good to remember that most other jamborees weren't as large and well regulated as de La Vega was. A lot of cats lived in jamborees that were more just *all the cats who live in the area* but without a real structure.

"I think the initiative Kendra is heading up is something of great use to us as well."

Kendra, Max's wife and the other Alpha of the jamboree, was also a witch and was bringing a whole lot of change into their culture, trying to unite in the face of a rising threat.

Unity was a good thing. It made you powerful. And the more powerful you were, the less people considered fucking with you. It wasn't always a clean job, and there were things Gibson had had to do that he'd regretted, even as he knew he'd had no other choice.

"Can't hurt to reach out to the other jamborees more often. Cross train other Alphas, other Bringers and seconds. Avoid this stupid shit." Max sat back in his chair.

"We'll find out one way or the other soon enough. Regardless of their reasoning, we'll have underlined a painful lesson. Ten is unreasonable. For any jamboree."

"Keep an eye on them. I'll let you know what happens when I finally connect with their Alpha." Things were tense enough as it was without any inter-jamboree crap. He knew Max had a lot to manage and yet, his brother had risen to every single challenge.

Gibson nodded. "You should let Kendra do it. I love to watch your woman get tough." He said it, knowing his brother would be annoyed, knowing it would ratchet the tension back as well.

"She told me today that she'd rather deal with third graders than jaguars. Said third graders were more mature." A smile lurked at his lips as he said it.

"She's got a point. Anyway, I've got stuff to do. I'll check in once we know they're gone for sure. You know where I am if you need me." He stood and then bowed to show his fealty.

"Appreciate the service."

Mia Porter finished her last pull-up and dropped to the ground. The muscles in her upper body burned with exertion. The sweat cooled her skin, helped her get past the ache.

"Excellent work today."

Mopping her face, she could curl her lip without being seen. She was so over this freaking injury and all the physical therapy that came afterward. She wanted to be what she was before.

"Thanks," she said instead of punching her therapist. He also happened to be ridiculously hot, so it didn't seem fair to snap at him when he looked that good and was only trying to help.

"You're really doing well. I'm impressed with your progress. Give yourself a few more months and you'll be back to a hundred percent."

"No. I'll never be back to the place I was before."

He sighed. "You're correct. But you'll have the full use of your right arm back and you'll be able to rock climb again." He leaned against the wall. "I know it's not what you imagined for yourself. But you could have died. You didn't. You're here, a month after you were attacked, a few weeks after you were released from a hospital where you were in a coma, and you're doing pull-ups that a majority of my fittest clients couldn't do. I know it's not on your schedule, but you're pretty exceptional. Just give it time."

Attacked seemed a very mild word for the hate crime she'd endured, but she let it go because it didn't matter anyway.

"I'm going to hit the showers and go home. Thanks, Rich, I'll see you tomorrow."

She'd been decorated three times while serving in Iraq. Two purple hearts for being wounded and a combat medal her entire unit was awarded. She'd served her country and done her part. Mia was proud of her time in the military, damn it.

She survived a place where people tried to kill her pretty much every day only to have come home and settled in Los Angeles post-military. And then a month ago she was hauled off the street into an abandoned building, beaten severely and left for dead.

Had it not been for the women who'd seen her and called for help, she might have indeed died. Shifter blood or no, her attackers had used silver on her so the wounds were slow to heal and the damage to her muscles would be lasting.

That they used silver was a clear indication she was attacked simply for being a shifter. Which still chilled her to the bone.

Knowing she was attacked for what she was burned in her guts every time she thought about it.

She had been living in Los Angeles, but her family was in Boston. How would she get to her physical therapy and other doctors' appointments without them? Her mother had been sure to drive home that particular point. And as usual, her mother had been correct.

And to be honest, she missed home. Missed her old friends and family. So, she'd come back to Boston and had started looking for a new place. Her older brother was away for several weeks so she was crashing in his apartment while she hunted for a place to live and while she figured out what the hell to do with her life. She would *not* let these new limitations stop her. She would climb again. She would get her strength back. She'd be able to fly again. Though not the heavy stuff most likely.

And just maybe she'd find a way to track down the assholes who'd done this to her and make sure they didn't do it to anyone else. The police were on it, but there'd been no breaks in the month since it had happened and she was beginning to think she'd have to do it on her own.

Not the first time really. She wound her hair into a bun before she gathered her things and headed out. Maybe she'd stop at the Italian deli near her brother's apartment. The impracticality of having to hide her identity as a shifter sucked, but the metabolism part did not.

So she was a little caught up in the decision between meatball and salami for her sandwich when she scented not just other shifters, but gun oil. Instantly alert, she scanned the area so when the shots went off and a car sped off, her training kicked in and she sprinted to where a man lay on the pavement, keeping low, her phone in her hand.

The scent of his blood hit her hard. A shifter. She put the phone away. No calling the cops for that unless there was no other choice. She crouched, taking him in.

"They fucking shot me," the large male on the ground in a pool of his blood managed to say as he tried to sit up.

"Stay still," she barked as she ripped the front of his shirt open. He'd been shot at least twice that she could tell. First the bleeding needed to be stanched and then she needed to get him off the street. She pulled her extra shirt from around her waist to press against the wound, and the blood stung her hands when it soaked through the material. Silver. "Shit."

"Ouch! Why are you shoving me down? I'll be fine in a…" His words trailed off and his eyes rolled back. A flash of memory hit her, disorienting her a moment until she ruthlessly shoved it aside.

"They used silver. Obviously I can't call the cops, but we need to get you off the street so I can dig the slugs out before they finish the job and kill you." She knew all too well just how badly *that* hurt. "My apartment is just a block up the street. Let's get you inside so we can call your Alpha." Though since she was also a jaguar in Boston, his Alpha would be hers as well.

He started to argue but she ignored him, hoisting him up on her left side, letting her cat surface enough to power her to that door. Damn, he was solid and heavy, like a freaking truck.

She took a chance that the elevator would work as she punched the button for the fourth floor. It shuddered a moment and squealed, but they did arrive safely and she hustled him to her apartment.

"Don't get blood on anything. My brother is pissy about that stuff." She managed to get the door unlocked and him inside.

He focused narrowed eyes on her. "You're a cat. Did you come in with the others?"

"I know it hurts but don't snarl at me." She laid a blanket over her bed with her free arm before she put him on it. She rustled through her things in the closet until she found her kit. She didn't bother with gloves—they were both jaguars and he was going downhill very fast.

"Did you come with Bertram's cats?"

"Who the fuck is Bertram?" She pulled her belt off and put it between his teeth before she got to work digging out the first bullet. "This is going to hurt."

He growled, his cat glowing in his eyes, watching her warily.

"What's your name?" Keep him conscious.

She ignored the complaining muscles in her right hand as she had to work to keep the wound open to dig out the second bullet. His body continued to try to heal around the wound, fighting her.

"Gibson de La Vega."

Oh wonderful.

She dug out the second bullet and realized there was one more just below the waistline of his pants. "Three times? You must have really made someone mad. I need to turn you over. This last one is too deep." She did it as she said it, not wanting to waste time.

She cut his jeans off quickly when she couldn't pull them off fast enough. The last bullet came out, the wound already ugly.

The poison would already be rampant in his system. The bullets she'd removed would have also exploded silver through him on impact. At this stage, what he really needed was to let his cat take over. The shift would cleanse his system.

It'd be far easier if he did it nude. His boxers were easy to pull off and set aside before she leaned down close to his ear. One of the ropes of his dreadlocks brushed against her cheek. Her cat responded immediately, rising at the scent of another cat. A male cat. A hot male cat. Enough of that. Still, he came out of his stupor a little as she'd hoped. "You need to shift. It'll help with the healing."

Shirtless, his tats showed against the dark chocolate of his skin. She'd seen the pierced nipples when he'd been on his back. Dreads. She'd been halfway across the world and this was the most badass thing she'd ever had in her bed. She tried to pretend not to look at his ass, which was quite honestly a thing of beauty. Hard and muscled like the rest of him. He was nearly unconscious after all—it wasn't like he was going to know she was objectifying him or anything.

She only knew of one other way to bring his cat besides having his Alpha right there to do it. And since she didn't have Max de La Vega's phone number on speed dial, there was one option left open to her.

Chapter Two

Those cats of Bertram's shot him. *Motherfucker.* Getting shot really pissed him off. Getting shot with silver? Oh, he was going to beat some ass when he recovered.

Rage roiled through him and he let it for a few moments, feeding off the energy. But it wasn't sustainable. Especially when he heard her voice. A little sultry. Unafraid *of* him though a little concerned for him. He winced as he tried to open his eyes, but it was hard. It hurt to breathe. The silver in his system burned, clawing through him.

The voice sharpened and he strained to hear. Change. Yes. She told him to change.

He should do that.

He got his eyes open and then couldn't look away as he caught sight of her. She was getting naked. Her shirt came off, exposing a no-nonsense sports bra and a seriously in shape torso. Then her jeans were off, socks and the barely there panties. Until she was utterly bare. But before he could focus on her further, she shifted.

Her cat's energy filled the room with the magic of the change. His own rose in response, and the tug in his gut was enough to grasp and get his cat to come.

The world changed all around him. Scents, powerful but still muted in human form, burst through his senses. He was strong and cunning. He would be safe now because he was feared and respected.

The pain slowly wisped away and his blood sped the exorcism of the poison. His system burned it up. Destroying it.

Within a few minutes he'd healed enough to notice other things in the room. The female, most especially.

His cat liked the way she looked. Small. Golden with delicate rosettes all over her fur. She head-butted him and he sent her a lazy growl. Here in her place, he had no desire to do anything but lie and watch her. Breathe in her scent.

He head-butted her back, letting his teeth catch her a little. She responded with a growl of her own before swatting at him, her claws still sheathed. He knew this female would draw blood if she were truly unhappy. His cat liked that too.

She stared at him and blew a frustrated huff.

The human within wanted to change back. Needed to check in with the Alpha and find the people who harmed him. The cat did not care. It just wanted to be here in this place with this female.

She changed back slowly, easing to stand as she grabbed her pants. He scented the pain, just a brief twinge, but it concerned his cat enough to let go so the human could surface.

"Are you all right?" he managed to say as he rolled to get to his feet. The wounds had healed over but still hurt. The cost of using silver.

She stepped into her jeans and zipped up before sending him a look over her shoulder. That's when he saw the freshly healed wounds on her chest.

"Me? *You* got shot three times with silver. I'm fine." She pulled a T-shirt on, not bothering with a bra.

She tossed him his shorts. "I had to cut your pants and shirt. I'll get you something of my brother's. Your phone is right on the nightstand if you need to call someone." She sashayed from the room.

He grabbed it and called Dario. "Hey. Turns out Bertram's cats wanted to shoot me. Three times. With silver ammo. I'm all right, but I want some men out there now, looking for these cats. I want them brought in to answer for this."

"Are you all right? Do you need a healer?"

"I'm fine. Someone helped me. Another cat. Get on the search and call me back."

And then he followed up with a call to his brother.

"Max is listening to your mother give him a lecture right now. What do you need?" Kendra barely held back a snicker.

"I told him that if he didn't take care of that fence issue the way she wanted she'd skin his ass alive." She had such a lightness to her tone that he hated to say the next part. "I got shot tonight."

"What? You did what? Are you all right? Where are you?" She'd gone from scared and concerned for him to bossy all in one sentence.

A tussle as Max must have heard and came to take his phone back. Kendra clearly allowed it, as Gibson heard no howls of pain. And there would have been if she hadn't wanted to give up the phone.

"Where are you?"

His savior came back with a shirt and some sweats.

"Where am I?" he asked her as he pulled the sweats on.

She rattled off an address that he didn't bother relaying to Max, who'd have heard it the first time.

A fact his brother underlined when he began to give orders in the background before turning his attention to Gibson again. "Sending a car now. We'll have a doctor for you. Do you need the hospital? Who are you with?"

"She's one of ours. A cat." He turned his attention back to the woman. "You never said what your name was. At least not while I was conscious."

She looked him up and down as she decided to tell him or not. "Mia Porter."

Well, shit.

"Did she say *Porter*?" Wariness edged Max's voice.

She sighed. "Yes, that Porter family."

"How do you know she's not part of it?" his brother asked.

The brown of her eyes went amber as her cat rose close to the skin. He liked that. Though the look on her face was scary enough that he'd give her some space.

One hand on her hip, she snarled in response to Max, and Gibson was glad he got to see the glorious fury of this female. "You've got some nerve to make accusations while your brother's blood is all over my sheets. Get this straight, asshole. My family may not love yours, but if I wanted anyone dead, I'd come straight on and do it so you knew it was me."

Gibson liked some moxie in a woman. This one had that in spades. Too bad she was a Porter. "He didn't mean it like that."

She rolled her eyes, totally unimpressed by his name, or Max's, for that matter. "Of course he did. Your grandpa wasn't all that. Just a serial cheater with a swelled head. Not rare and not special. Dumb assholes getting shot and when you help them they accuse you of being part of it. How do I know you didn't need getting shot anyway?" When she pointed a finger in his direction, her breasts jiggled a little bit. Enough for him to lose his train of thought a moment.

Max cursed in the background. He wasn't usually this clumsy when it came to dealing with the cats in his jamboree, but he'd touched a nerve and Mia Porter was one pissed-off woman.

He tried for a sexy smile, most likely watered down by the blood. Though she was a shifter so maybe not. "I probably do merit it." He spoke to Max again. "But this is Bertram's doing. I scented his cats before I went down. I've got my men on it. I'll be over in a bit." He hung up and took in the wreck of her room before he went back out to the living room in her wake.

She favored her left side but was clearly right-handed, and he remembered the freshly healed spots on her chest and arm.

"I'm sorry about that. He didn't mean it, not the way you think. He'd have asked the same thing of any other person who happened to be around."

"Clearly you seem to think I'm unaware of how your family runs things. I know how he meant it. Just like I notice he didn't ask the question until he heard my last name."

He sighed but didn't argue because she was right in part.

"Did I hurt you?" He tipped his chin to indicate her right side.

Something passed over her features before she put it away. "No."

"The person who did it? He still alive?" He hoped so, just so he could kick the shit out of a person who'd hurt her.

She handed him a glass of juice. "Plural. And yes, unfortunately."

"Silver?" Everything in him stilled.

"Among other things, yes."

"Want my help with that? The alive part that is. I'm feeling a little mean just now, so making someone pay for hurting one of my cats would hit the spot." He hoped he sounded casual, because he felt murderous.

She laughed but wasn't amused. "There'll be a reckoning someday. And when it comes, it'll come from me."

Even preoccupied with this situation with Bertram, he couldn't help but be impressed by Mia Porter.

"Porter or no, not many people would have gotten involved much less dragged a man back to their apartment to dig bullets from them. I appreciate it." He sat.

"My mother didn't raise her children to ignore a dying man in the middle of the sidewalk. Even if you interrupted my plans for a meatball sandwich for dinner." She was moving slowly, clearly favoring one side.

"Are you all right?"

"Not all of us come from an alpha family." She raised a brow but when the buzzer sounded, she sighed. "It takes a while for me to recover after I shift." She turned to answer. "Yes?"

"I'm here for Gibson."

She buzzed the door open. "Second floor. Apartment C."

He was a pretty big guy and he must have been dead weight. She'd brought him all the way back up here from where he'd been shot? Even as a shifter, she had to be extra strong to handle it. "Thank you. I, uh, ruined your bedding. I don't have a wallet with me but I'll reimburse you."

She waved it away, and he would of course ignore it and do just what he wanted.

Lauren Dane

He opened the door before Dario could knock. "Mia, can I contact you again? I might have some questions about what you may have seen."

She looked him over warily before giving him her cell number.

"Thank you again. I'm in your debt."

She shook her head quickly. "No. I keep telling you, there's no debt for doing what's right."

Damn. He liked this one. Too bad she was a Porter.

He nodded. "All right then. Thank you again."

Dario looked him up and down as they got back to the street. He tossed Gibson the keys knowing he'd need that control.

"Max thought it best to send me. I put Robby on the search."

His brother was smart that way. "Good idea. First let's go back to where I was."

They walked over, finding the spot easily enough. Dario combed through the bushes in front of the small park and around the apartment buildings lining the street. "Large cat prints."

The place stunk with Bertram's cats. "I'm beyond understanding here." He stood, stretching a little, the wounds from the shots still burned, though they were healed over on the outside.

Dario took a call, turning his attention back to Gibson. "Craig and Emmy connected with Robby and Matt. They're working together to track the cats now." Robby and Matt were the two from his team that Gibson had sent out to escort Bertram and his cats from town. Craig and his mate Emmy were also on his team and some of his best hunters.

"What's the story then? I know I didn't mumble when I told them to stick with Bertram's cats until at least the state line."

Dario knew there'd be hell to pay if someone had messed up. Gibson was pretty laid-back unless his orders didn't get followed. And if they weren't, he underlined just why he was in charge to start with.

"They followed them to the state line. They checked in with me at that time."

A raised brow as Gibson thought a moment. "So they waited and turned around to come back? Foolish, no? I want Bertram Simmons and I want him as soon as possible. I don't give a fuck if he's got to be dragged back here by the scruff of his neck."

Bringing an Alpha from another jamboree to show obeisance was unusual. And maybe if they hadn't *shot* him he'd have more mercy. But this was nothing less than a declaration of war and de La Vega demanded answers.

Gibson would get those answers.

He got back in the car, and they headed over to Max and Kendra's where he was quite sure half his family would already be waiting.

"You got shot? Gibson, what did I tell you about that?" Imogene opened the door mid-lecture before she hauled him into the foyer, looking him over with a mother's eyes.

No matter that he was the most feared Bringer in the country, that gaze took him right back to about seven years old and he had to resist the urge to make an excuse.

"It's not like I wore a sign around my neck saying *shoot me*." He frowned, but his mother was made of far sterner stuff than to even give the look a second glance.

"Mami, let him get inside." Max came out and put an arm around their mother as he shot his brother an apologetic glance. "Come through. Kendra's worried and I want to hear the whole story."

Kendra looked up from her screen and came over. "I won't fuss. But I'm glad you're all right. Sit, and after you talk business, someone is totally going to tell me who this Porter family is and why it's all so *escandalo*!"

Max heaved a sigh, but Imogene laughed. Kendra lightened Gibson's heart. She was perfect for his overly serious older brother. She made him laugh, poked at him and didn't take him too seriously. Max's leadership was only enhanced by her at his side.

"Look, I met with Bertram's Bringer this morning along with his human lawyer. I set them straight on what the rules were and then told them to get out of our territory before calling to get the permission they needed to be here. I checked in with Max when the meeting ended. I had my people follow them to the state line. I thought it was over. Apparently not."

"They used silver. It's not even an overreaction, it's just totally nonsensical. We've never had beef with them. Hell, they're some tiny little jamboree. I don't think I've dealt with them at all before this." Max ignored the sound of their sister-in-law Renee entering the house along with their brother Galen, and Galen and Renee's other mate, Jack.

Renee walked right up and hugged him tight before kissing both cheeks. "This isn't good. I am not a fan of my best boys getting shot. Gibson, did you look too good to someone's wife or something?"

Kendra, who also happened to be Renee's sister, laughed. "Dude, there's some other mystery too. Porters, whoever they are, are involved."

Galen shot him a look.

God. Women. "Let me finish the story before getting to the Porter thing." He told them the rest of the story, all he knew anyway, and then turned to Kendra and Renee.

But before he could say a word, Renee shoved a mug of something mildly stinky into his hands. "First drink this. It'll help with the poison the silver left behind." He should have known better than to have assumed he'd get away without some of her potions. She was a healer. A nurturer. He pretended to be annoyed, though she touched him with the way she cared for the people in her life.

Of course it tasted like the bottom of a shoe, so he gulped it down and fought back the grimace he wanted to make.

"Cats using silver on each other. What is the world coming to?" His mother nearly growled.

"I don't know what this is all about, but if I don't get answers and very soon, I'm going to have to get mean." Max began to pace and his wife watched him carefully.

"Let me tell you the story of the Porters and de La Vegas. Cesar's father and his brothers were all very close. Jorge, that's Cesar's father, took over jamboree leadership from their father when he was a pretty young man. His right-hand cat was his next oldest brother, Silvio."

Imogene, warming to the story, took Gibson's hand before she continued. "Silvio had an eye for the ladies." She rolled her eyes. "Legendary, even for a de La Vega male. He began to court one of the cats in the jamboree."

"Oh uh oh, I can see where this is going." Kendra shook her head.

Imogene nodded. "Indeed. Lettie was one of the most beautiful women in Boston in her day. Still packs a punch in her seventies. Lettie's parents went to Silvio's family, the alpha pair, and demanded they either make him back off or get serious about their eighteen-year-old daughter. Who he got pregnant."

Gibson sighed. He really hated this story. He wondered if Lettie was Mia's grandmother or great aunt? Wondered too, what she had been raised to think about his family.

"Of course he had to marry her. It wasn't so long ago that a boy who got a girl pregnant would marry her because that's what you did. Especially in a tight-knit shifter community. Wedding plans went forward, but a month before the date Lettie lost the baby. But they didn't cancel the wedding. He made his bed and he made it with a young woman he got pregnant. Cesar's father was beyond old school. He was an old-school shifter. The day of the wedding arrived and the church was full. Full of everyone but Silvio and one other cat, a female by the name of Charlotte."

Kendra's features left no doubt just how outrageous she thought Silvio's actions were. "He left her at the altar? Please don't tell me he went to Vegas to marry Charlotte."

"Not Vegas. But he ran off with her for several weeks, and when they came back, they were married and she was pregnant with the first of three children she gave him before he imprinted on yet another female he ran off with for good. Abandoning his wife and kids back here."

Kendra shook her head slowly. "Wow, that sort of is a scandal. So the Porters clearly hate the de La Vegas for a reason, though Silvio isn't here anymore."

"It gets worse. He and Charlotte spent a great deal of time talking poorly of Lettie when they returned. Charlotte, who I do like, couldn't ever really get past her jealousy of Lettie, so she was quite unpleasant on that subject. The Porters pulled back, though they never left the jamboree entirely. They attend major gatherings and answer all the calls made. But they don't do anything more than what is required. Jorge made amends with them I know, but there's an enmity to this day."

"Whatever the current state of de La Vega, Porter drama, Mia carried me back to her apartment and saved my life. Quick thinking."

"Cesar and I plan to thank her ourselves. She did a great service to this jamboree and to my family."

He barely managed to keep his cringe inside. "I don't know if she's going to like that."

"It was two generations ago. Ridiculous to be held back by that man whore Silvio's dastardly deeds." His mother waved lazily. She'd clearly made her mind up, and he had nothing to do but hope it went all right.

He tried to push to stand, but his mother put a restraining hand on his shoulder. He reined in his impatience and squeezed her hand. "I need to get back out there. I want these cats found and dealt with. Nobody shoots me and walks away without a lot of pain."

Imogene simply kept her hand in place, one brow arching.

"You'll do no such thing. You will nap for three hours at the very least, and you'll do it here so we can keep an eye on you." Renee stood and Galen sent Gibson a look.

The look told him he was on his own.

He gave Renee a smile and cocked his head a little. "*Bebe*, really I'm fine."

"No you aren't." Her response made him frown. This is what love got you. Bossy women. He had enough bossy women in his life but his brothers kept bringing more home.

Renee waved away his expression. "You have silver in your system. It's a poison, remember? You need to rest to let your body get rid of it all. Once you've rested and are back to one hundred percent, you can go hunting. Don't give me your *grr* face, it doesn't work on me."

Kendra nodded and moved between him and the door. His mother shrugged and gave him a little push toward the stairs. "So, you'll nap and eat before you go back out. Go on up, the bed is made."

With a barely restrained sigh, he got up and trudged past his brothers, neither of whom seemed to have a damned bit of control over their wives.

Renee put a hand to his cheek, and he paused to let her fuss a little before he moved up the stairs and toward his old room to take a nap like a cub for God's sake. He hid a smile as he gave one last look at them before the stairs curved out of sight. If anyone outside the family ever found out what a total marshmallow he was for the women in his life, his cred would be shot to shit.

Chapter Three

Mia looked up from the counter at the sound of the chimes. Imogene de La Vega came in. Mia only knew this was the former alpha female because she'd long admired the woman's sense of style when they'd attended the very few jamboree events her parents had allowed over the years.

Imogene wasn't the type of female one forgot.

She shot a quick look to the landing where her father was explaining the difference between two bottles of Malbec to a customer before she headed to intercept Imogene. Hopefully she could handle this before anyone even noticed.

"I'm looking for Mia Porter." The expression Imogene wore told Mia the woman knew exactly who she was speaking with.

"That's me."

Imogene looked her up and down and nodded once. "I'm pleased to meet you." She held out a hand and Mia took it automatically. She didn't offer her throat or any other submissive behavior.

"I'm Imogene de La Vega, and I wanted to come and thank you in person for saving my son's life. I apologize that it took me three days to get here."

Surprised by the visit, Mia nodded. "I imagine your schedule is fairly busy. You're welcome. I did what anyone else would have. Is he all right?"

"As you might imagine, or maybe not since you don't know him very well, but he got some sleep that night he was shot and then got right back to the search for those who shot him. He's hard to keep down. Even when he was a baby he just never stopped in that gruff, taciturn way he has." Imogene paused to look Mia over carefully and it made her a tad defensive.

"Did he find them?"

Imogene shook her head. "Not yet. But my children are steadfast. Gibson won't give up until he's successful. People like those who harmed him can't understand that. Would you have some time? Perhaps to get some coffee across the way?" She indicated the tiny Cuban coffee stand on the corner.

"Really, it's not necessary." She lowered her voice. "My grandmother will be by later. It would be better if you know"— she paused, trying to find the politest way to put it—"you weren't here."

"It's been over fifty years. What happened was wrong, but it looks to me like she got a much better deal. She built all this with your grandfather. I think it's silly to hold a grudge this long. Don't you?"

Mia knew she whipped her head a little, but her grandmother had suffered a lifetime's worth of sorrow at the hands of the de La Vega family and that wasn't silly. It was fucked up beyond measure, and it had turned her grandmother into a stone-cold bitch who loved her family fiercely.

"Of course she got the better deal. As for it being *silly*? She was an eighteen-year-old girl who within just a few months of her life fell in love, got pregnant, got engaged to the man who fathered her baby...and then she lost the baby, her fiancé left her at the altar and ran off with another woman. And then when he got back, he spent his time spreading the most vicious of gossip about her. She lost everything. Her friends felt that they had to choose the side of the jamboree leadership. They wouldn't speak to her at all. Her family lost everything—their business and their home. Because they couldn't get supplies their customers stopped working with them. They were nearly destitute when she met my grandfather."

Fate of course, her grandmother insisted and dared anyone to argue otherwise. Lettie loved Seamus Porter with the same intensity she showed for everything else. She said those two years had hardened her enough to make a success out of her life and build a family. Even today her grandmother lived the hell out of every moment.

Seamus Porter was a ham-fisted Irishman who also happened to be a jaguar shifter. He'd been in Boston visiting some cousins when he'd bumped into Lettie on the street outside a bookstore.

He married her four months later and, from that moment he'd bumped into her, had loved her like she was precious. In their fifty years together they'd had four children, eight grandchildren and one great-grandchild. There was no doubt Lettie got the better deal.

And yet, it was all bound up with what her entire family had suffered. The tragedy had shaped her and it wasn't always pretty.

"So no, no I don't think what she endured was silly. What I think is ridiculous is that you'd have the audacity to come in here and call my family silly for being angry over something like that. So, nice to meet you and all but you should go."

Imogene actually smiled, and Mia knew why she made a powerful leader who even her family admitted ran the jamboree well. Her charisma was large and vibrant. It was impossible not to respond to the blast of her energy. If Mia hadn't been there in the shop, surrounded by her family, the people she was protecting, it would have been impossible not to look down faster. But she still did after a tense moment.

Imogene released her immediately. "I like a girl who defends her family. It was a stupid turn of phrase. I apologize. What I meant is, I'd like to see if we can deal with this and put it away. It's been a long time. What happened to your grandmother and her family was wrong. It'd be my pleasure to have you all be an active part of our jamboree once again."

She pulled a business card from her bag and handed it to Mia. "Please call me for lunch. I'd like to talk with you about your future." She turned and left, head held high.

It was impossible not to admire that sort of confidence.

"Care to tell me why Imogene de La Vega was just here?" Drew, her younger brother, asked as he came into the shop from the back.

"Were you hiding?" She laughed.

"She's scary. But I wasn't hiding, I was letting you handle it. So why was she here?"

"I told you I dug some bullets out of someone." She shrugged.

"What? I thought you were full of shit. You dug bullets out of someone in Joe's apartment? He's going to pop a vein."

"You really thought I was making that up just to mess with you? As for Joe, he's not going to pop anything. Unless it's because once you open your mouth about the bullet thing, it'll only be fair to let him know it was you who put the crack in his windshield when you *borrowed* his car." Joe was away for a month, which was good or he'd have smelled the blood she took so much care to clean up after Gibson had left that night.

"You're diabolical." He knew she didn't make threats lightly, and he sighed, flipping her off as he scratched his nose.

She snorted. "You're an amateur. Thank God you're so pretty." Mia grabbed the stack of cards she'd made for the weekly staff recommendations and began to put them throughout the store.

"It was a good idea." He shrugged. "The cards and the tasting nights. Business is up. And I know they love having you here again. You should stay. What do you have out there in LA anyway?"

That was a good question. "I have to figure this all out. I can't work here. They can't afford it." Drew was the manager at the shop. Her parents ran the place. They didn't have the kind of profits to bring her on full time.

"You can find a job. You can do everything and better than everyone else, so what's the real issue? Do you hate us?" He teased but she realized he might not have been entirely convinced that wasn't the case.

"I love you all. It wasn't a difficult thing to come back here." She paused, watching his posture loosen a little. "I'm thinking of going back to school to finish my degree." She'd left UCLA to join the air force after several years of wandering. It had made her feel special, like she was doing something. Gave her the chance to use her love of flying those big, heavy supply runs.

"Why not fly? You have a license. You're an amazing pilot."

"I don't know if I'll ever recover my strength. I can't pin my hopes on that. Anyway, an engineering degree is totally useful. I can pay for part of it with my GI Bill money."

"Sure. Except you don't want an engineering degree or you'd have one already."

She frowned as she placed the cards. It was silly to not be practical.

"What is it you want to *do*? You have this time to figure it out, you know? Take this shitty thing life gave you and make it into a plus. If anyone can do it, you can."

"I wanted to be a pilot. I wanted to rock climb."

"And so you say you can't be a pilot now, though I don't believe it. You can't fly a giant cargo plane anymore. But that doesn't mean you can't fly other aircraft. You can fly anything. You're one of those people who just does it all well. So do it and stop wallowing. I've never seen you wallow, it's ugly on you."

She sniffed her annoyance but didn't argue. In truth she did really need to figure out a direction and go with it.

Being insightful, he got it and backed off a little. "So did you get, like, the jaguar medal of bravery for this bullet digging out? Is that why she came to visit? Add it to the chest full of stuff you've got already?"

"It was her son I saved. They used silver on him. Shot him just feet away from where I was. She came by to thank me personally. Said she wanted us back. That they wanted to have us be involved in the jamboree again."

Drew's brows rose. He was dating a girl from a family who was far more involved in jamboree events, so as a consequence, he went as well and found he enjoyed having that sense of community with the rest of the cats in their area. He'd been trying to talk their father into going, and it was currently a sore spot between them.

"I appreciate the thank-you and all, but I didn't do it for that. I did it because to do anything else would have been wrong."

"Of course you did. It's who you are. Anyway, so which son was it? One of the good, single ones or one of the dick losers?"

She laughed and socked his arm. "Gibson. Didn't seem like much of a dick, or a loser. Though he was an alpha through and through, so dick is there in his DNA anyway."

He grinned. "The Bringer. Stacy's brother Dario is one of Gibson's guys. Thinks pretty highly of him. What are you going to do? About the visit and what she said?"

"I'll talk to Mom about it later today."

"How's physical therapy going?"

She harnessed her snarl of annoyance. "It's fine. I'm fine."

"And you don't like being asked every day, but I don't like that you pretend getting attacked was nothing big. You were victimized, Mia, and I don't think you should feel any shame for being affected by it. You don't have to be perfect all the time."

"Oh look, a customer." She moved past her brother, ignoring his comments, and headed to the couple who'd just come in. She didn't want to talk about it. She was sick of thinking about it.

Was it too much to just want to get back to normal?

She took in the couple who'd entered the shop. Cats. Interesting, but not totally unusual. A long time had passed since her grandmother's days, and many of the jaguars they knew shopped there. But these two she'd never seen before.

Something wasn't right. It was more than them not being familiar. It was the way they held themselves. She flashed back to the faces of two men who'd been wearing a similar expression as they'd walked into a crowded marketplace and set off a suicide bomb. She'd been behind a low wall. It was what had saved her life. Two of her escort had not been so lucky.

Shit. Shit.

It was as if time slowed. The man shoved his coat back and pulled out a weapon, and her training simply took over.

"Weapon!" she shouted as she sprang into action.

His bones gave way when she grabbed his wrist and twisted to make him drop the gun. Mia landed on his chest, knees at his throat, a snarl on her lips. The woman had run out the door.

"Who the hell are you?" she shouted over the ringing in her ears. Her thigh oozed blood, but the flow was already slowing. No silver then. At least there was that.

The male hardened his mouth into a grim line, his face pale.

"Do you think I'd hesitate to hurt you again to get an answer? I'm not a human, I'll cut you just to watch you bleed." To underline her point, she popped him one and let the crunch of a broken nose assuage her rage a little.

But he remained close-mouthed until Drew got to them and hit him so hard it knocked him out. "Stop wasting time." He frowned at her.

She socked him in the gut. "I was questioning him!"

"You're bleeding. Again. Let's deal with that *first* and then we can question him."

Her father arrived, first aid kit in his hands.

"What the hell is going on? Your mother wants to call 911."

"No! Let's see what the damage is first."

Her father's face was pale as he dealt with the wound in her thigh, and she tried very hard not to wince. "Clean through. At least we've got that much." He packed it, enough to hold until the wound began to close on its own.

"No silver, which seems dumb. Why Gibson and not me?"

Drew narrowed his gaze. "You think this is connected?"

"What are you two talking about?" Her father's tone was taut. He was on the verge of losing his temper in a big way.

"How could it not be? Doesn't it seem like far too great a coincidence? Two shootings in the span of a week?" She quickly explained the situation to her father. Being as brief and non-scary as she could.

"Why does it not surprise me that de La Vegas are involved? It would be very nice indeed not to have to deal with people trying to hurt you. Also, your knowledge of silver versus non-silver ammunition does not fill me with confidence over your well-being."

"No kidding, Dad." Did he think she wanted this? Her life before this was not filled with danger and silver bullets. "These were new pants. Jerk."

She managed to stand and her father moved her straight to a nearby chair and his look dared her to argue.

"Stay still for God's sake! Let your body take care of it."

"Should we call the cops?" Drew stood after binding the still-unconscious man's hands.

"We can't." She knew what she needed to do, which didn't really make it any easier. "Take care of your customer, Dad. I'll deal with this. Drew, put him in the broom closet after you hogtie him."

Thank heavens the customer was a long-time one and a cat as well. Made her call a little easier when she didn't have to worry about hiding what had happened or why she wasn't bringing in the police.

She got voicemail that was as gruff as the man himself.

"This is Mia Porter. Two cats entered my family's shop and one of them shot me. We have him here, bound and locked in a closet. The other, a female, got away." She hung up and turned back to the shop where her father returned from letting their customer out the side way.

She busied herself by cleaning up the mess until her father bodily put her in a seat.

"For heaven's sake, Mia! Sit down and rest. Since we're alone, you can tell me what's going on. The full story because I know what you told me was just a sliver of the whole thing. Is this related to what happened to you in Los Angeles as well?"

"I don't think so." She sighed and told him about helping Gibson three nights before.

His brows were high and he shook his head. "My darling girl, you never do anything halfway, do you?" He gave her an affectionate, slightly befuddled hug.

"Go big or go home, I guess. Anyway, I called Gibson, so hopefully he'll get back to me soon. I don't want to keep a hostage all day long. Even if it would be fun to break and re-break his nose over and over."

"You used to wear dresses and play with dolls. I preferred that." Her father frowned.

"Can't be seven forever." Her phone buzzed in her back pocket, freeing her from having the same old conversation.

"Are you all right?"

It was Gibson. He had a very growly voice. She liked it. Her cat responded immediately, and she tamped it down as well as she could under the circumstances and hoped fervently that her father didn't notice.

"Interestingly enough, not the first time I've been shot. Anyway, I'll be healed by tomorrow."

"Hmm. I'm across town but we'll be there as soon as we can. You didn't call the authorities?"

"Only the furry one who just told me he was on his way."

He paused, clearing his throat. "So you recognize my authority?"

She knew she blushed but she couldn't help it. "Enough to call you when a jaguar comes into my family's store and shoots me."

He laughed then. "Sit tight. You have him confined in some way?"

"Yes. He's in a closet. My brother hogtied him. Drew was an Eagle Scout so he's awesome with the knots. Plus he knows how to keep a shifter bound. Extra points I suppose."

"Hold tight. Shoot him if he moves. Don't let him get away."

"I broke his nose already. I'm thinking he gets that I'll mess him up if he tries anything else fishy."

"Yes, okay. On the way." He hung up.

She brushed a hand down her leg and winced when she came upon the bandage. A good reminder. This wasn't the senior dance for God's sake.

She turned back to her father and brother. "The Bringer is on the way."

Chapter Four

He didn't bustle in. Didn't barge or storm. No, Gibson de La Vega seemed to melt into the space. How he did that and still managed to be a total badass she had no idea. But it made her a little dizzy. He moved like a male on a mission, his gaze taking in every corner, every place anyone could be standing or hiding.

But when that assessing gaze caught on hers, it was like everything held its breath for a moment. She had to gulp at the immensity of the way he looked at her. It was more than the usual shifter gaze. This male was big and dangerous, but *hot damn* was he delicious.

That gaze moved from her face down to the place where her leg had been doctored up. He frowned, moving to her. "Are you all right? Shouldn't you be resting?"

She shrugged, fighting shyness she didn't know the origin of. "I'm fine. I'll be healed tomorrow. Missed the bone and all major arteries."

"It's not acceptable."

It was a laugh that surprised her then. She couldn't help it. He was offended by how she healed?

"Well, that's tough. It's how I heal."

That gaze again, those deep brown eyes boring a hole right through her defenses. "The getting-shot part. Not the healing part. Silver is hard on even the fittest shifters."

"Oh." She wiped sweaty palms down the front of her jeans, wincing when she got near the wound. "They didn't use it. It was 9mm ammo. No silver."

He cocked his head. "I wonder why that would be?"

Dario shifted. "What's their game?"

"A good question for our prisoner. Where is he?"

"Here." She indicated the closet. "He's in there."

"Can you lock up? I don't want anyone wandering in. I need to...question him." He did stalk this time, right up to the closet.

She threw the locks on the one door she'd left open. She'd closed up shop a few minutes before, not wanting to have to explain why they had someone tied up and held in a broom closet.

She was steady. Alert. Holding herself together well. He couldn't imagine too many other shifters who'd be doing so well after being shot.

Admirable.

And even so, Gibson seethed with rage. It wasn't something he did very often. But the very idea that this female had been injured by anyone, much less this trash of Bertram's, was offensive beyond the pale. Shifters didn't go to war with other shifters. Not now when they faced such big outside threats. They should be standing together, not shooting women. Not harming *this* woman.

Her brother, that much was easy to deduce given the strong resemblance, nodded his way. "I'm Drew."

He didn't hold a hand out though. He showed his neck and averted his gaze, accepting Gibson's dominance. So very unlike his sister in that way it nearly made Gibson smile.

Instead he nodded.

Dario grinned and tipped his chin. "Hey, Drew." Dario looked back to Gibson. "He's dating my sister."

He thought he recognized the face from a few jamboree events of late.

"Let's get this trash taken out."

Drew opened the door, and the male jaguar was still tied up but was conscious and pulling at his bonds. Gibson reached in, grabbed the rope and hauled him out, tossing him on the floor nearby. "Who are you and why are you here?"

The jaguar just looked up at him.

Gibson sighed and leaned back against the counter. "I have no plans to scare you with threats. I will shoot you if you don't answer my questions. That's not a warning, and it'll be the only time you hear it before I unload a few bullets into you."

Fear bled into the guy's eyes. Good. Fear was useful.

"You shot one of my cats. You also shot me. What's the purpose here?"

"My name is Hal Pepper. I'm acting on my own."

Gibson pulled his weapon and clicked the safety off.

"If you shoot a hole into those floors, my dad is going to kill me." Mia spoke from beside him. "Can't you just kick him or something? Blood is easier to clean up."

He allowed himself a smile.

"Kicking doesn't seem to get the message across. Shooting is far more effective."

She nodded. "This is true. Just aim for a place on him that the bullet won't pass through. I told you, the floors. They're original, did you know that? Well, if you spend five minutes with my dad, you will. For months and months he was obsessed. He redid them all when they first bought the shop years ago. He's not entirely rational when it comes to his floors."

The guy on the ground whimpered and she rolled her eyes. The smile wanted to get bigger but he wrestled it back.

For Hal, Mia only had derision. "What are you crying about? You shot *me* remember? I'm not crying. If you walk into someone's place of business and go shooting, you can't be upset when you get caught and hogtied, later to be interrogated by the Bringer. Jeez."

Dario's lips trembled but he held it together. Gibson didn't meet his eyes or he'd have laughed.

"You shot a cat in my territory. Why?"

"She annoyed someone."

Mia barked a laugh. "I annoy lots of people. Very few of them end up shooting me. I don't even know you! I'd remember if I annoyed you enough to get shot."

"So much for I'm acting on my own." Gibson leaned down, rapped the guy with the butt of his gun to knock him out. "Take this filth back to a holding cell. We're going to leave him alone for a few hours. No one is to speak to him." He gave Dario some more instructions, trusting him to get the ball rolling.

Dario hauled the cat up over his shoulder and left.

"I'd like to speak to you about this. Do you have the time?"

She looked him over carefully. "All right. You can give me a ride home."

Given the way she looked like she needed to eat and nap, he'd add some dinner in to the mix too. "Drew, thank you for your service. The jamboree will see to it that you're reimbursed for any time you had to close today and any damage caused by the bullet." He shot a look to Mia. "And any medical bills you might incur."

Drew laughed. "It took being in a coma for her to seek medical assistance. Getting shot isn't going to do it."

Then he yelped when Mia punched his arm. "Hey, Chatty Cathy, don't you have plans?"

Drew rolled his eyes at his sister and left the room.

"You're sort of scary."

"Says the male who just threatened to shoot someone."

"You're not afraid of me."

"I'd shoot you back." She raised one shoulder and his cock twitched happily. Stupid penis. She was *not* appropriate for him.

"You need to eat as well. Consider it part of the fee I owe you. I have a place I think you might like if you're a meat eater."

"That'll do."

He allowed her to open and then lock the door after them and ushered her to the car. Dario had taken his back to the building where they'd house the prisoner.

She took in the SUV. "Nice. This could be in a movie about guys in dark sunglasses charged with protecting the president or something."

He opened the door for her and would have helped her up but she had an expression that told him he'd be in danger if he did.

"I don't need dark sunglasses with the windows so tinted. But I do protect the equivalent of the president."

She shrugged and he caught sight of that leg again. "At least let me see the wound."

"I'd have to take my pants off for that and you haven't even bought me dinner yet. In fact, stop by my apartment so I can change. I can't very well go into a public place with bloody pants."

If she'd been intimidated by issuing an order to the Bringer of her jamboree, she didn't show it. And God help him, he found it attractive.

He found a place to park near her building. "I can carry you. It's not a big deal. If your leg hurts too much, that is."

She opened her door and slid to the ground, and he sighed, getting out to join her.

"It hurt for the first half an hour. Now it's just a dull throb." She unlocked the outer door and they went inside.

Once in her apartment, he noticed several things. It smelled like a male lived there, which made him frown. He had the idea it was a relative, but he wasn't quite sure why.

She shuffled into the bedroom and shut the door behind her. Her leg did hurt, though she wasn't going to say so. He'd been shot three times and was up within twenty minutes. She could deal with a thigh wound, for goodness' sake.

Only it was hard to peel the pants off, and she had to get into the shower to do it. And then of course she fell with a yelp and cracked her elbow on the tile.

Which would have been embarrassing enough. Until he burst through the door, a snarl on his lips, his teeth bared. And she, laying naked from the waist up, her pants now wet and tangled around her calves.

"Get out! Jeez!"

"Are you all right? Did you fall?" He ignored her orders to leave and helped her to her feet. Then he knelt to get a better look at the wound, which wasn't bleeding at all by that point. But his breath on her skin and her state of near nakedness made her want to giggle. Or hit him. But she resisted both.

"It's looking like you're healing well. Have you changed?" He stood and looked at her breasts. He wasn't supposed to do that. Shifters were pretty nonchalant with the naked thing. But this wasn't a casual perusal. This was a boy-type person looking at her boobs.

"I was trying to, but then the pants got stuck to my skin because of the blood and you didn't mean my clothes."

"I don't think you should go out. I know of several restaurants nearby who'll deliver."

Then he started getting naked.

"What are you doing?"

"You need to change and then you need to clean up. Once that's done, we'll get you some protein and rest with your leg up so you can heal better. And during that you can tell me the story of what happened today in your shop."

She'd planned to argue, but he grabbed her throat. Not to hurt, but to collar and get her attention. And boy did he get it. But not as a cat. Her nipples hardened, and the rest of her was equally pleased by the action.

Too late to blush.

A smile curved one edge of that mouth up, and she shivered and licked her lips.

He growled, but it wasn't a scary one.

He was...well, he was a whole lot of male and holy shit did she like it.

"You need to change. Let your cat heal you." He got very, very close, his teeth grazing over her shoulder, sending a shiver of delight through her body.

At least as a cat she could stop blushing. She let the change come over her. The world of her cat reigned now. Scents, especially his, tickled her senses as the wound on her back leg tingled. She stretched, rumbling her enjoyment when the man slid a big, strong hand over her head and down her throat. He spoke in human words and she ignored all but his tone. Her cat liked his tone.

He knelt and looked into her face. The words he spoke brought the woman to the surface, brought her back, the pain of such a quick change pricked her skin.

"There you are." He helped her up. "Better?"

"You're almost naked." She was queen of random today, apparently.

"I was planning on changing with you. You seem to have issues with authority, and I knew my cat could bring yours. But you surprised me by obeying."

"How about you leave now so I can finish this shower? There are takeout menus in the drawer under the phone." She nearly managed sarcastic. But they both knew her heart raced.

He took one last, lingering look and sauntered out, his clothes in his hands. "Try not to fall again. You have enough injuries for one day."

He went back out to her living room, sucking in some air that wasn't choking with her scent. That sweet, tangy scent the man and the cat seemed to want to roll around in.

Zipping his jeans up over his cock was painful, which helped him get his control back after he'd lost it and tasted the skin of her shoulder. Stupid. Because now she was inside him and he wanted more.

He shouldn't have touched her, even to get her attention, by taking her throat. He'd started to do it to get her cat to take over. But once he'd touched her, once his shirt was off and his jeans were halfway down and he got close... Well, once that happened he was in a whole world of hurt.

Of course, her response only made it harder to resist taking their contact to another level. Her pulse had sped, her pupils had swallowed all the color of her irises and her breath had stuttered. She dug it as much as he did.

He scrubbed his hands over his face to get it together again.

Digging through the drawer she'd indicated led him to a really good Puerto Rican place he quite liked. He ordered enough for six or so people and waited for her to come back out while he gave up on not thinking about her body.

She was small, probably barely five and a half feet tall. Her hair was a little darker than honey. Hazel eyes. They'd been more brown the night he'd met her, but today they had some more green. A sweet nose and freckles. He was a sucker for freckles.

She was lean and toned, with tits barely more than a handful, but perky. Goddamn he loved perky breasts. Mainly because women liked to go braless when they had boobs like that.

He also took in the evidence of the coma her brother had alluded to back at the store. She'd mentioned an attack back that first night. Something terrible had happened to her and he wanted to know more.

She was a beautiful, scary, sexy woman and he liked that a whole hell of a lot.

He might as well call in while he waited. Maybe talking to Max would help him think about something other than the way she'd licked her lips, or the way her skin felt against his lips, against his teeth.

Christ. *That* sure wasn't helping at all.

He dialed his brother.

"What's the story?" Max answered, without any preliminaries.

"I've sent the cat to the holding cells. Gonna sweat him a while. Says his name is Hal Pepper. Sounds like a fuckin' character from a Dr. Seuss story. Dario is having Galen look into it. He shot Mia Porter in the thigh. Clean enough. Went clean through. The woman he was with left the scene. But they have surveillance footage. The brother will forward it to my office so we'll see if we can't figure out who she is too."

"Do you think this is related?"

"At first he said he was acting alone. Then he said she'd pissed someone off. Probably by saving me. I don't know for sure, but it's awfully coincidental, don't you think? Two cats in the same jamboree shot within the span of a week? And the second shooting victim is the person who helped the first one?"

"I don't believe in coincidence."

"No. Me either. They didn't use silver though. With me they did. This was 9mm ammo. Enough to do a shitton of damage, even kill her if they'd hit her hard enough and in the right places. But I don't know why they'd use it on me and not her."

Max heaved a sigh. "I connected with Bertram's second. Not his Bringer. Claims Bertram is in South America right now. Also claims to not know anything about this incident. I find that hard to believe."

As did Gibson. At that point, he suspected everyone having anything to do with the Smithville jamboree.

"Where are you?"

"I'm questioning Mia. She's in the shower right now."

"Your definition of questioning must be vastly different from mine."

Ha.

"She got shot in the leg. It bloodied her clothing."

"Don't even think I don't know you smiled when I said that. Keep me apprised." He hung up. Max knew Gibson would ask for help if he needed it. His brother let him do his job, as their father had before him. That was a source of great pride.

He wandered around the living room, pausing to look at the photographs. The place smelled like a male, but it was clearly someone she was related to. The resemblance was strong, just like it was with Drew.

There was a vague memory of her saying it was her brother's place.

She'd been a pilot. He knew part of the story because he'd had a quick check of her done after he'd met her. But he saw pictures of her, medals on her chest, and it hit home. What had happened to her after she returned?

He spoke when she came out of the bathroom moments later. "I ordered some Puerto Rican food. Should be here shortly." They'd known the phone number and the address so he took a guess that she ordered it frequently.

Simple delight rode over her features, making her beautiful. "Yes, that works."

She'd braided her hair back from her face, exposing her features. "I like your hair like that." He frowned momentarily, not having had any intention of saying that out loud. "Are you feeling better?"

She shrugged. The blush she wore heated her skin, sending her scent through his senses. "Better than I was an hour ago, sure."

"Sit and get that leg up." He pointed to the couch, more gruffly than he'd intended.

"You're imperious, aren't you?"

But she did it.

"You have two brothers, right?" He leaned forward to tuck a pillow under her knee before sitting down across from her.

"Yes."

"So the bossiness of shifter males isn't something new to you."

"Not new, still annoying."

"Difficult." He sniffed. "Did you recognize the cats who came into your store today? Have you ever seen them before?"

"No. They came in and I noticed they were shifters. I thought it was funny that I didn't recognize them. We have regulars from the jamboree." She sounded nearly defensive and he felt bad anew about what had happened.

"You're not shunned, of course you have regulars from the jamboree."

She rolled her eyes. "Anyway, no, I didn't recognize them."

"What about from the other night? The night I got shot. What did you scent that night?"

"Cats first. There aren't so many of us around here that it's something I scent very often. Then the gun oil."

"And then the shots?"

"Yes. Three pops. I was less than half the block away from you. They ran, but you were on the ground. I didn't know if you were alive or not."

"You made the right decision." She'd already described the area to him in detail the night of the shooting, but it was good to go over it again. "Tell me about what happened. With the coma."

She looked him over carefully. "It's a really long and boring story."

"You should let me be the judge of that."

"Why? Why do you want to know?"

Why indeed? She was not for him. He had a job to do. He should leave and go do it.

"Maybe I want to know you."

"Why?"

"You have trust issues."

She laughed, this time she was delighted. "I do. My mother told me all about boys like you."

It was his turn to laugh. "Like me?"

"You know. Bad boys. And you're like, well, like five or six all at once. I bet you own leather pants and have a motorcycle."

"I wear the leather when I'm riding."

She threw her hands up. "Exactly. Cripes."

"What does this have to do with anything?"

"Take a look at yourself. You are a supreme badass. Boys like you want girls to put out and why the hell not! You move like you know a lot about what to do with a lady's best parts."

He cocked his head. "And you don't like...putting out? Because, I have to tell you, Mia, despite my better judgment I'd like to get all up in what you've got."

She nearly choked and then the buzzer sounded.

He stood. "Food's here."

He smiled once he turned his back. He'd succeeded in getting her nice and befuddled. For whatever reason, this amused him greatly. And it's not as if he'd lied. He wanted her.

He paid for the food, and when he'd returned to the living room, she'd set the table. "I've got water, juice, milk. The basics."

Of course she drank milk. She was wholesome. Which also made him hot.

"You shouldn't have gotten up. I'm capable of putting food on a plate for you."

"I'm sure you are. But you and I both know you're going to need me to go down to jamboree headquarters to look at pictures and whatever else."

He'd been thinking that. Well, aside from the way he'd been thinking about fucking her. He had some pictures of the cats who'd come to their offices earlier in the week. He wanted to know if she recognized any of them. But he'd been thinking of having Dario bring the stuff to her place.

"You're injured."

"It's fine. You can drive me there and I'll cab it back."

He frowned and sat. "You'll do no such thing."

She ignored him as she opened boxes to check what was inside.

"They had your last order in their system. I just doubled it and added a few things."

She loaded her plate. "Thank you."

He was the one who needed to be thanking her. She'd gotten involved in this mess, most likely, because of him. And she didn't seem resentful about it. He might have been in her case.

"So, you don't like bad boys?"

She piled black beans on a tortilla before she glanced his way. "I didn't say that. I said my mother warned me about them. You're one."

"Am I?"

She took several bites. He'd tried dating human women a few times. But he didn't like having to hide who and what he was. This female though, well she was thoroughly a Were. She ate with gusto. Moved with that predator's grace shifters sometimes had. She was a warrior too.

"Your mother came to the shop today."

He looked up quickly and Mia laughed. He had to admire the way she changed the subject so well.

"She was gracious and I think I avoided having a death sentence put on my head. I just remembered she'd come in. You might want to check in on her. She could have been the target."

His phone was in his hand before he was even thinking about it.

She answered on the second ring. "Hello, Gibson. I hear we had some excitement with the Porters today."

Of course she'd have heard already.

"Yes. I'll brief you about it later. Mia told me you'd been in today. I wanted to be sure you were all right."

"I went in to thank her. As your mother and as jamboree leadership. She's quite something. Is she well?"

"She's been shot. But no silver." This time. "I'm feeding her and then we'll go down to the offices so she can look at the pictures we've got of Bertram's cats. I want to see if she can ID any of them."

"Can't it wait until tomorrow? She's been shot, Gibson. Let the girl rest."

Mia snorted and he had to fight his smile.

"I'd suggest it. But you met her today." He didn't say more.

His mother's laugh was delighted. "Yes. I imagine she'd tell you she was fine and to just get on with it. See what you can do to get her and her family back involved with the jamboree. I think it's well past time for it."

He didn't look up to see Mia's reaction to that.

"I'm going to have Dario put some extra eyes on you. On Papi too."

His mother sighed. "Fine."

Mia liked that he called his father Papi. It was sort of adorable without being creepy.

She frowned as he finished his call to his mother. She'd tossed the visit out there to get him to change the subject, and now Imogene was trying to get him to do her dirty work. Their whole family was sneaky. Which was a quality she generally admired. But it meant most likely he'd turn that let's-have-sex face on her again, and she was not strong enough to resist.

She knew her flaws. He was beautiful and masculine and really freaking hot. That in and of itself was hard to say no to. But he was a shifter, like her. There'd be no hiding. No holding back. Which...well, sounded pretty good, but she didn't need this sort of complication.

Did she?

She shook her head, hard. No. She did not. She needed a nice, quiet life. With a nice male who didn't carry sidearms and look broody.

Even if looking broody only made Gibson look sexier. Which seemed impossible. But it did.

"You're deep in thought."

"Just about what I'm putting on my plate next."

He snorted. "Sure. And I'm driving you over to the building to look at some video. The cats who attacked me and the ones who attacked you seem connected. And they seem connected to an event that happened three days ago. I don't want to color your opinion more than that at this point. And then there'll be no cabs. I will bring you back here myself."

"Hm."

His features went wary. It was clear he had some experience with strong women. His mother was one, after all.

"Hm isn't a yes, but I'll take it as one. You should just be glad I don't put a bodyguard on you."

This time she simply looked at him for a few heartbeats. "I think not. I'm perfectly capable—"

"Of getting shot in broad daylight. These cats aren't running on a full deck. They're acting way out of character."

"Why? And why me?"

"Maybe they saw you helping me. Maybe they think you know something. The problem is that I don't know enough of anything right now and I need your help."

Oh. Well.

She nodded. "I'll help if I can. But I didn't see anything that night."

"You smelled it though."

That was true.

"Take your time. There's no rush. I'm leaving that cat in a cell overnight."

"Where he'll have hours and hours to think over what you'll do to him. Diabolical."

Gibson nodded.

"You're scary."

He smiled at her, just a brief glimpse of those white, white teeth. Goddamn, she really, really wanted to lean in and bite him. Somewhere. Anywhere. His bottom lip would be a good place to start.

Wrong. Wrong. Wrong. This was a de La Vega. He was not on the menu.

Chapter Five

She looked through the video twice and then pointed at the screen with her pen. "That's the woman who was in the shop earlier. I don't recognize the male though."

He took notes. The female she'd pointed to was a low-ranked cat. She hadn't even come into the room when he'd met with the Bringer. No wonder she'd run at the first sign of trouble.

"Have you seen her before? Before today?"

"I don't think so. Who are these cats?"

"They're members of the Smithville Jamboree. Near Nashville."

"What's their beef?"

"What makes you assume that?"

"Let's see. I'm not stupid. You got shot. I got shot. You know, the types of aggressive behavior that don't normally just happen for kicks, but usually comes from motivation." Her smile was bright, and Dario studied the floor carefully, a smile flirting at the corners of his mouth.

"It was a stupid move." He explained the issue about bringing so many into their territory without asking and how they'd had to be escorted from de La Vega territory.

"If you did that—I mean, without Max's permission—what would happen?"

"That's not something healthy for a Bringer to do."

"Clearly then, it's motivated by some slight or something someone in the jamboree did, or was perceived to have done to one of their cats. This isn't random. It's not stupidity. It's still stupid, but the acts are on purpose as a response to something they think you did."

"Ostensibly. But I can't get in touch with their Alpha. He's out of the country."

"Convenient."

He thought so too. And he didn't like it one bit.

"Will you wait for me outside? I'll be with you shortly and get you home. I just want to speak with Dario a moment."

She stood and he didn't fail to notice the way she kept her weight on her left side. She was still in pain, and he wanted to get her home as soon as possible.

She left and he turned to Dario. "Anything new?"

"Nothing. Galen pulled up some stuff on this Hal Pepper guy. He's from Tennessee. Nothing about the jamboree, not that membership in a paranormal organization is such public news."

"Call Bertram's second. I want this answered for and I want those answers now. I'll go down there if I have to. They really shouldn't make me."

Dario nodded and Gibson knew Dario would make that point.

"No one in to see Hal. He's not to make calls or any other kind of contact. I'll be back in the morning to question him. I'm going to get Mia home. Call me if anything comes up."

He went out to catch her at a window, looking out over the city.

"I missed Boston. When I was in Iraq. And then when I was in Los Angeles. I wanted to be home."

He walked with her to the elevator and then down to the garage. "I've traveled a fair bit. But I'm always happy to come back here. Shitty drivers and all."

She smiled. "I rarely drive here. I just take the T everywhere."

He hoped she did less of that while these cats were out and about.

"Leaves you exposed."

She snapped her seatbelt. "Public transportation? Probably. But I know how to defend myself."

"What did you do in the military?"

"I was a pilot. Supply mainly."

"That where you got hurt?"

"I got hurt in Iraq several times. Lots of people shooting at you, all the time."

He remained quiet as he pulled out onto the road and headed back toward her building.

"The attack happened in Los Angeles. A few months after I'd been discharged."

She stared out the window and he wanted to touch her, reassure her. He was sure it was tied in to her being one of his cats. After all, his family had run de La Vega for generations. That's all it was.

"Hey, Gibson, there's a car following us."

He forgot about her skin for a moment. "What makes you say so?"

"Headlights. Same shape and size. Following us from the building and through the last three turns you made."

He kept an eye on the car she'd indicated.

"How'd you learn to see if you were being tailed?"

"I can't say I knew much at all until Iraq. Now I know." Her laugh was rueful.

"Were you ambushed?"

"More than once."

And then she braced her arms. "We're going to be hit. Do you have a weapon?"

He turned, and saw the car coming toward them. Toward her side of the SUV. So he sped, maneuvering between traffic and narrowly avoiding the crash.

"Glove box. It's loaded."

She pulled the Sig out and checked the clip.

"Turn left up here. If you go around the park you can bypass the congestion up ahead."

He obeyed, knowing she was right.

He ordered his phone to dial Dario and told him where they were and what was going on.

"Later-model Jeep SUV. Bronze. Charlie, Tango, Racetrack 145. Man at wheel is white male. The tail appears to be a sedan. An Audi. Nice taste your violent little friend has." She spoke as she continued to scan the area.

"Did you get that?"

Dario had and would be running the plates.

Then she reached out, shoved his head down and shot right through the space where his head had been. She grabbed the wheel and wrenched it hard toward her. "Speed up!"

The back of his SUV got clipped but because she'd taken the wheel and moved them enough, he was able to get the car to the side.

And then she got out!

Fuck. Fuck. Fuck.

"Damn it! Mia, get back here." He kept low, following her out her door, keeping the car in between them and their attackers.

"Listen, I'm no one's target. Got me? No one's victim and no one's target."

"There are bystanders all around."

"So call the cops. But you can't and the problem still exists."

She stood and stalked toward the car, her arm with the gun in her hand extended. Her face was a mask and it sent a shiver through him.

The car reversed in a hurry and she squeezed off three shots, all hitting the car as it sped off.

"Well then." She put the weapon in her waistband. "I got the license plate for that one too, but I think it's stolen."

He hauled her close. "Are you out of your mind? What do you think you're doing?"

"Not laying down for anyone else to kill me." She paused and sighed. "You're bleeding. Come on. I can bandage you up at my house."

"Mine is a few blocks away."

"Fine. Shove over and tell me where. We'll get there while you call those plates in."

Which is how he ended up with her in his house.

She cleaned up the cuts on his arm and forehead as he remained as still as he could. Which was hard enough when she was so close. He just wanted more. Wanted to lean in and sniff.

He tried to think about the situation. Piece it through. If he focused on that maybe he'd stop thinking about her naked. He should have had Dario come to the house instead of giving him the information over the phone.

It was just the two of them now.

"They're already closing up. You have a very fast metabolism."

"That was some really quick thinking back there." Without the way she'd simply taken over, they'd have ended up in a pretty bad car crash. The chances were good they both would have been all right, but she was already injured enough. Not to mention the not-so-small problem that there'd been passersby who'd have been even more endangered that way.

"Your window was already halfway down. I'm sorry you got cut."

"I can survive. Especially when worse would have happened if you hadn't been so smart."

And then he wanted her. Wanted her more than he'd wanted anything in a really long time.

She stood between his thighs as she'd been tweezing the glass out of a wound on his shoulder. He made her dizzy. Which was also part of the adrenaline, she knew. But it was him.

His pheromones changed. Surged and then sort of blanketed her in warm, sexy hotness. This was... Well, she'd never had this before. Her arm throbbed, her leg throbbed, and she really should sit down and rest. But she was rooted to the spot as one of his hands slid up the back of her thigh and came to rest, cupping her ass.

The heat of him blasted against her chest as his scent rose to her nose. His dreads brushed against her bare arm. His cat was just barely leashed, but he vibrated with all that self-control.

He tipped his head back and her breath caught.

She shouldn't be doing any of this. But she dipped her head just that small amount to meet his mouth and that was it.

He surged to his feet, his free hand joining the other, cupping her ass to haul her closer. Not that she minded. He was hard against her. A mass of man and muscle that nearly sent her to her knees.

Which, all things being equal, wasn't a bad next step.

His taste slid through her. Her cat approved of his, approved of this man with his hands on her ass, his tongue in her mouth, teeth grazing her lip until she gasped and he growled.

He opened his eyes and met her gaze, and it shocked her into total stillness. But when she freed herself, she nipped his bottom lip like she'd wanted to earlier.

He'd been nearly back under control until she grabbed his bottom lip between her teeth and tugged as her fingers dug into the muscles of his shoulder, hanging on and driving him right back to the edge of sanity.

He exhaled and tried to let go of her ass but found it impossible. His cat wasn't having any of it.

She moaned, her fingers relaxing, no longer digging into his shoulders, but didn't make a single move to disentangle herself from him. His cat eased back a little, but he kept that luscious ass in his palms.

"Where you goin'?"

She swallowed with some effort. "Where do you want me to go?"

He groaned, tugging her close enough to grind his cock against her. "What do you think?"

"I want you to say it."

He smiled, mainly because she had a spine of steel and he liked that about her. But also because she knew what she wanted and she demanded it.

"I want you to go into my bedroom so I can get you naked."

"Was that so hard?"

"It is, yes. I hope that penchant for demanding your due extends to fucking."

It was her turn to smile. "Fuck me and find out."

He bent his knees and picked her up, adjusting his hold on her butt. She wrapped her legs around him as he carried her into his bedroom and put her down carefully on his bed.

"I'm not fragile."

He snorted. "You got shot today. If I break you, how can I fuck you?"

She whipped her shirt up and over her head, tossing it across the room. Her bra followed, and she shimmied from her shoes, socks and jeans. "That's true. You're not naked."

He remedied that while he watched her get totally naked. Not bothering to hide his hum of satisfaction as she slid the panties from her legs and lay back, her gaze roaming over his body.

"You're something else." He got on the bed, kissing the pink parts on her chest and shoulder, and she shivered.

"I was about to say the same."

Her fingertips traced over the muscles of his back as he kissed over her collarbone and watched her nipples stand at attention.

"The piercings are so hot I can't quite stand it."

He stretched to take her mouth again and she pressed her body to his.

Skin to skin, she gasped at how good it felt, and he swallowed the sound. He smelled good and felt even better. He kissed her nearly senseless. The scratch of his facial hair only made it better.

She pushed him back and got to her knees to look down at him. He was…holy shit he was amazing.

"You shouldn't put your weight on that thigh."

Smiling, she threw one leg over his body and straddled him, resting her weight on his thighs.

"I like this view." His gaze moved from her face down, down and straight to the heart of her.

"What a coincidence." She flicked her index fingers over the piercings in each nipple. He hissed and writhed a little so she dipped her head to lick over first the left, then the right. He seemed to enjoy that so she filed it away for later. "Love the tats." His chest was broad and hard with muscle. Her hands slid over warm, taut skin as his gaze never left her. It was…disconcerting and yet really exciting to have him watch her the way he did.

He was a predator after all. But so was she!

But not with him. With him she was his prey. This made her shiver a little.

"Are you cold?"

"No. Just…delighted."

A flash of his smile in the dark.

She tugged on one of the ropes of his hair. "I like this too."

They were to his mid biceps, and they added to the overall badass vibe. Tattoos, muscles, dreadlocks and enough smolder to send a girl's underpants up in flames.

She kissed down his neck, pausing to breathe him in at the place where it met his shoulder. Which in retrospect had been stupid because his scent bounded into her system, sending it into overload. Her cat surfaced, pressing against the human skin it wore, and his responded.

He groaned and flipped her, shielding the side she'd been shot on. "That's better. Now I get to slide all over *your* body and kiss all your parts."

And he made good on that promise, starting at the hollow of her throat. He kissed, nibbled and then licked, tasting her pulse. More kissing across her collarbone and over the healing scars from the attack. She shoved it from her head and just enjoyed it. Especially when he moved a little farther down and found her nipple.

Unable to tear her attention away, she watched as he licked over her nipple. Slow at first and then he sped up to flick before he sucked it between his teeth. She was sure she should have been embarrassed by the sound she made, but she couldn't bring herself to be.

She held on as he found her other breast and did much of the same to that nipple.

By this point she was so wet and ready she rolled her hips to get his attention.

But it wasn't until she dug her nails into his shoulders and growled that he let go of the nipple long enough to meet her eyes.

"Yes?"

"Fuck me!"

He laughed and kissed his way down her belly, insinuating his body between her thighs. "I need to be sure you're ready first."

She was totally ready. But it wasn't going to stop her from enjoying that first long lick of her pussy. Or the second. By the time he made the third one she'd dropped her protests and let her head fall back to simply enjoy what he was doing.

On and on he went with that mouth of his and devastated her until she was shaking so hard it felt as if she shattered into a thousand pieces when she came.

"Holy shit."

He chuckled and kissed her belly. The slide of his hair over her skin sent her back into sensory overload.

And that was before he nudged at her gate before pushing in so very slowly. Thick and meaty, good gracious he filled her up. So much to enjoy about this male. She opened her eyes to find him above her, his face a mask of concentration.

Her vision was good, even in the dark of the room. Enough to see the bunch and ripple of his muscles as he began to thrust in earnest.

His eyes opened and met hers, and everything stilled. He saw right through. Right into the heart of her, which was freaky even as it felt right. Freaky enough for her to wrap her uninjured leg around his stellar ass and pull him in deeper to break his concentration.

He fucked her hard and deep, each stroke slow and deliberate. He took his time, demanding her response, which she gave. She rolled her hips to meet his thrusts, tightening around him, giving him a little swivel until he growled.

Smiling, she stretched up to lick over the biceps so close to her face. He tasted so damned good she hummed with it. Which reminded her she hadn't been able to taste him.

Perhaps she'd do it next time. If there was a next time. It was only fair.

He watched her below him, her hair spread around her face like honey. Her tits jiggling perfectly as he fucked her. She was so tight and hot around his cock that he'd worried at first he'd come three seconds after he got inside. And then she'd added that swivel and he'd nearly lost his composure.

She was small but strong. Toned and nicely flexible, even with a freaking gunshot wound on her thigh. She pulled him deeper with her calf, urging him on with the prick of her nails on his upper arm.

Her taste was still on his lips when he licked them. He needed more. More of her. More of this. A female who was as unabashed as this one was a treat on just about every level. Porter or no, he had plans to do this again very soon.

And when she added a back-and-forth movement as he got all the way inside, he knew it was nearly over. His control was frayed and just about worn through. Her scent drove him wild. The heat of her body, the sweet taste of her skin when he leaned down to lick over the swell of her left breast brought his cat closer to the surface. Hers was there as well, but she didn't try to hold it back. She threw herself into fucking, opening the way between them, letting him in, letting his cat and hers mingle in that space just beneath the skin.

That was all it took. One last thrust and he came with a snarl, holding himself deep and trying not to rest any of his weight on her right side.

He rolled off with a sated sigh and she laughed, moving close.

"Yeah, I'm feeling a lot better."

He rumbled a laugh against her face as she rested on his chest.

Chapter Six

The last thing she expected to see as she approached her apartment was Gibson de La Vega standing there with an actual smile on his face.

"Hey. Hope you don't mind but I was in the neighborhood. Would you like to grab a bite somewhere so I can give you an update on what's going on?"

She smiled back. "I'm totally starving."

He walked with her a few blocks to one of her favorite little Japanese places. "Do you like Japanese food?"

"I haven't eaten it very often. But I'm happy to try it if you'll give me a primer on what's best to order."

He was being very sweet.

"Are you sure? There's a great pizza place just across the street if you'd rather."

He opened the door. "No. Really I'd like to."

The server gave him a long look and showed her boobs to them far more than was proper, but he kept his attention on her as they watched the food move by on a conveyor belt. She ordered hot tea and turned back to him.

"I sort of lied," he said when she began to pull plates off for them to share.

"How so?" She mixed some wasabi with soy and then did it for him as well.

"I don't really have an update. But I was in your neighborhood and I was hungry, so I thought I'd stop by."

He made her flustered like a teenager. "Well. I'm glad you did."

He tried several different kinds of sushi, really enjoying the eel and the tuna.

"Tell me about your life."

"That's a huge subject." She grabbed some more tuna.

"All right. What are you reading right now?"

"I'm reading Vaclav Havel's *Living In Truth.* It's a collection of his best essays. He's amazing. One of my idols. What about you?"

"*Haunting of Hill House.*"

"Really? I loved that book! I haven't read it in years."

"When I finish you can borrow it. If you let me borrow *Living In Truth,* that is."

"You've got yourself a deal. Did you always know you wanted to be the Bringer? Was it like a family thing and you did it because you were supposed to?"

He sucked in a deep breath. "That's a long story. But the quick version is that yes, I did know. I was trained from a very early age to do it. It's something I love. Something I believe I'm meant to do."

"I like that."

"I feel very fortunate. A lot of people, hell maybe most of them, don't get to do things they feel born to do."

"The Bringer is the heart of the jamboree," she said softly, quoting the story.

And he was. The Bringer was justice, not vengeance. The Bringer protected and kept the cats safe. Guarded their rules and laws and found and judged the wrongdoers. It was a big job. One she wouldn't have wanted at all. Being judge and jury had to be pretty damned tough.

"I try very hard to do that justice. My mother would most likely spank me if I didn't. She's very smart that way. A judge in her own right."

She enjoyed that he respected his mother so much. From what she could tell, Imogene deserved respect and had raised at least one very decent son into adulthood, so that was a big reason to respect her right there.

They sat and had more tea and talked books for another hour or so until he walked her back home.

"Would you like to come up?"

"Yes, I would."

But his phone rang and he paused to answer.

By the tone she knew he was going to have to leave. Which bummed her out because she wanted to leap on him and jump his bones.

He put the phone back in his pocket. "I have to go." He shook his head. "Trouble back at work. I'll see you soon though. All right?"

She nodded.

He stepped close and pulled her to him, his lips brushing over hers once and twice before he settled in for a long, sensual kiss that left her weak-kneed.

"Bye for now, Mia. Be safe."

He held the door for her and she went inside. "You too."

And she watched him jog to his car just across the street, admiring that stellar butt of his.

She might have sighed wistfully.

"You're looking better than you have in a long time."

Mia looked up as her mother spoke. "Thanks."

"Apparently getting shot isn't the key. Does it have anything to do with how much time you've spent with Gibson de La Vega?"

She sipped her tea, thinking over what she'd say. There was something between them. Aside from the amazing sex, which would have been more than enough on its own. But it wasn't what her mother thought. She didn't even have time for what her mother thought.

"You make it sound like I'm with him every minute of the day. He's investigating what happened to me. I helped him after he got shot. It's not unusual that I'd be spending time with him. He's a nice enough cat." She shrugged.

Mia's mother snorted. "Of all the people on Earth for you to tell that story to, you think your mother is going to buy it? Plenty of nice boys out there, Mia. I'm not opposed to you finding one."

"Not looking for a nice boy. I'm not getting shot because I have a crush on the Bringer. Anyway, too much stuff on my plate just now. Dating is low on the list. I need to find a place to live and a job first."

"You have a job."

"Mom, you guys can't keep me on. I know there's some seasonable stuff now, which is why I'm happy to stay on for a bit. But we both know the shop is fully staffed with you and Drew. And I can't afford to work part time. Especially once the physical therapy ends."

"Are you going to go back to school, then? What is it you want to do with your life?"

She sighed. "I was thinking of finishing my degree."

Her mother shrugged. "Baby, you don't want to be an engineer."

"You're the mom. You're supposed to encourage things like engineering degrees. Good degree. Good prospects."

"You don't want to be an engineer. It's why you left school to join the military in the first place. I'm all in favor of you having a good, solid career, but I'm not a fan of you doing something you'll be unhappy with. Especially when you're plenty capable of doing something you do love. Like flying."

"I haven't totally ruled it out. But did you hear two airlines just passed internal rules that they won't hire werewolves to fly commercial? They said they're worried about any lunar stuff affecting their pilots even though of course that's not how it works. Lots of ignorance out there right now. How do you think they're going to feel about a jaguar-shifter pilot once we come out? Hm?"

"Those two airlines are stupid. As your father and I have discussed. Anyway, they're not the only airlines and you can do other sorts of flying. You can still fly helicopters and small planes. You have options, Mia. Don't let this attack mess with your head this way."

Mia blew out a breath. All of that was true. Shifters were often very good pilots because of their keen sight and senses and their excellent hand-eye coordination. But many didn't go into careers as pilots for various reasons.

"I'm trying. I have to get through the last bit of the physical therapy first. I've got a week or two of that left, and then it'll go down to only needing it once a week or so. Though I'll continue to work out with Rich. Whatever I do, if I keep on top of this

Lauren Dane

damage, the doctor said there's every reason to believe I'll get at least eighty percent of my original strength back."

Maybe by the time that happened she'd be able to accept she'd never be a hundred percent ever again.

Her mother's mouth flattened. "This is wrong, Mia. These thugs attacked you because of what you are. This is a hate crime. They need to be punished."

She nodded. "They should be, yes. But you heard the Alpha down in LA, he doesn't want to come out yet. There's all this other stuff with the witches going on now. He doesn't want to agitate matters."

"So they'll do nothing. Some alpha he is. None of them seems to give a tinker's damn what happens to their cats. Whatever is the point of belonging to a jamboree if they don't do anything for you?"

"They're not all that way."

It wasn't as outlandish to think so now. Gibson might be a de La Vega, but he'd done nothing but be protective of her since the first day they'd met. Albeit that was only a little over a week ago, but he hadn't tried to blow her off. And Max had called her about the gunshot to thank her for yet again putting herself in the service of the jamboree. He'd been pretty cool about it, even apologized for the way he'd asked if she was behind the shooting that first night.

"I will find the people who did this to me. And I'll take care of them."

She kept her mother's gaze for long moments, waiting to see any disappointment or anger and saw nothing but resolve. "You will."

And that was that.

And she still needed to figure out what to do with her future.

"Max, this is Bob Whitford from the Smithville Jamboree."

Max looked across his desk to Gibson before he answered. "Hello, Bob. You're on speaker with me. Gibson is here with Galen."

"Good, it's best they all hear as well. We've censured and removed Bertram as Alpha of the jamboree. I'm taking over."

Max's brows rose but he kept his composure. "Mind sharing with us what exactly happened? I assume this is about the attack on my Bringer and one of my cats?"

"Yes. Hal Pepper, his girlfriend Margret, the female with him, Bertram and two others have been removed from the ranks of the jamboree. Once you're done with Hal, if you decide to let him live, we'd like you to send him back our way. Margret is here, and if you like, you can question her, or we can turn her over to your custody. We don't want a war with de La Vega."

Of course they didn't. Gibson knew that. They were a strong jamboree. Stable, even with the betrayal of his brother Carlos. And now it was also well known that they had two witches in the jamboree. It added to the sense that they were not to be messed with.

"What's the motivation? Pepper continues to insist he acted on his own. We can execute him. After all, he did attempt to murder one of our cats in her place of business. But we'd like to know what the issue is."

Bob sighed. "No one seems to want to say anything. Bertram and these cats have been with this jamboree for years.

He's skipped, we don't know exactly where. His wife and their son are gone as well."

"What about the human?" Gibson asked.

"Human?"

"They brought a human lawyer with them when they came into our territory. What's his story and where is he?" Gibson had been looking for him since that first day, but he'd come up empty. The name he'd used appeared to be fake.

"I don't know. I...we have an attorney but it's a she and she's a cat. Why would we send a human attorney to deal with jamboree business?"

"This was our question. And I suppose now it's more along the lines of what prompted this mess."

"We have a new Bringer as well. I'll get him your info and have him look around and get back to you, Gibson. We sincerely apologize for what has happened in our name and ask that you not judge us along with Bertram and these other cats."

They'd be within their rights to call for war. Or to bankrupt Smithville. And depending on what they found out, it was still an option. But Max and Gibson, along with the other leadership, didn't feel like it was time for that yet. Not until they found out what was really going on.

"We accept your appeasement. For now. But we want to know what the fuck is going on."

"We understand and appreciate your patience. I'll keep you apprised. Understand things are up in the air here. The jamboree is...well we're all shocked. But this was not done on behalf of the jamboree. This was the crazed act of several individuals. We're trying to get to the bottom of it."

They spoke for a while longer before hanging up. Max turned his attention to Gibson. "So?"

"No use punishing all the cats in the jamboree if they had nothing to do with it."

Galen spoke up. "I've put our best investigator on this full time. He's got a team working. They're pulling together dossiers on all the cats we had here on the day of the shooting as well as on Pepper and the female he was with."

"Good. I want us working on this. I understand they need answers down there, but I don't give a fuck about that. My Bringer was shot with silver. For Weres to use silver on one another is an error we cannot allow to stand. And I'm sure as hell not going to stand idly by while my cats are being attacked in their businesses. I want answers, Galen. And I want them as soon as possible. The longer this goes on, the more tempted people might be to want to forget about it. That's not going to happen."

Gibson nodded. "The fact is, Smithville is a tiny, not very well managed jamboree. We can't expect them to have answers as quickly as we might. We have the structure and training in place for it. They don't. I'm not saying we don't need that information. At this point, I'm just not sure we're going to get it without a trip down there to do what they should know how to already."

Galen, who like Gibson was Max's second, stood. "All true. I'm working on my end. I'll see you both this evening at the gathering?"

Imogene had convinced Kendra it was necessary to have a dinner to honor Mia and her service to the jamboree. He'd tried to stay out of it, especially after the sex, but his mother had gone around him anyway, and whatever she'd said had convinced Mia to accept the invitation. She and her family were all invited, though he had no idea if the whole Porter clan would attend or if it would be just Mia. But he'd be at Mia's doorstep that evening. It was to protect her, of course. She'd saved him after all.

Gibson nodded. "I'll be there."

Max snorted. "Yes. Kendra and our mother have been working on the details. I'm just glad it's finally here so it can be over and I don't have to hear about it every day. And I admit to wanting to see this Mia Porter in person. Mami says she's beautiful." Max raised a brow at Gibson.

"That's an accurate description." He didn't smile, but he wanted to. She was indeed beautiful. He flashed on a vision of what she'd looked like spread out beneath him in his bed. And then later in her front entry when he'd made some stupid excuse to go to her place to check in.

"That's some loaded silence there." Galen winked.

"So, what's the story between you and Mia Porter?" Max asked when Galen had left.

"What do you mean?"

Max cleared his throat. "Really, Gibson?"

"There's no story. She saved me. Twice as it happens. She's clever and vicious."

"And beautiful."

Gibson shrugged. "Yes. And a Porter."

Max waved that away. "So what? She's not her grandmother and you are sure as hell not Silvio. Papi would beat your ass if you acted that way. I just... Well it's been a long time coming. You deserve someone. I don't care that she's a Porter and neither does anyone else."

"Look, we had sex a few times. I enjoy her company for what it is, but that's all it is. Something fun and casual. I respect her. But there's nothing more to it."

His brother just stared for long moments before he tapped his pen on the desk. "Stop lying to yourself. In any case, I'll see you later. Let me know what's going on with this whole Smithville mess."

Gibson stood, relieved to get out of that room and back to work. "Got it."

Mia adjusted her shirt a little. And tried to tell herself she didn't even care what Gibson thought of how she looked. A total lie. She blotted her lipstick and decided not to wear the bracelet she'd been considering.

A dinner in her honor. Good Lord.

When Imogene had shown up at the store, again, and proposed the idea she'd been really hesitant. It was best to keep away from jamboree stuff.

But of all people, it was her grandmother, Lettie, who'd been in the shop and overheard. She'd bustled out to give Imogene a piece of her mind about bullying Mia, but Mia had to explain the situation and her grandmother had cackled, laughing so hard she nearly choked. She'd patted Mia's hand, told her she was proud of what a fine woman she'd grown into and that of course they'd all attend the dinner.

Then she'd turned her attention to Imogene and told her that while she wasn't sure any de La Vega deserved to have silver bullets dug from them, that she was glad her granddaughter had more dignity than to step over Gibson and keep walking.

Imogene hadn't been offended at all, but rather, apparently delighted. The two had a back-and-forth that had left Mia cringing a time or two, but in the end, Lettie and Imogene had left the shop to go get coffee and that had been that.

She had no idea what her grandmother had told Imogene, but the invitation hadn't been rescinded so she figured it couldn't have been that bad. She'd seen Gibson that same night—she smiled again remembering just how she'd seen him—totally naked. But he hadn't acted any differently toward her either, so she made the assumption that Lettie hadn't drawn blood, or if she had, all was forgiven on Imogene's part.

Well, no time like now to get her butt out the door.

She locked up and then nearly punched Gibson in the face when he melted out of nowhere as she reached the sidewalk.

He put his hands up. "Didn't mean to startle you."

"Hmpf." She unfisted her hand and resisted patting at her hair, though she did run her tongue over her teeth just in case she had lipstick on them.

"I was thinking it'd be good to give you a ride over to the dinner."

"Were you now?" As if she didn't know he wanted to do it himself because he liked to be in charge.

"Better that than the T. And you look so pretty you know you'd get harassed." He looked down to her feet and raised a brow at her.

She had on some pretty peep-toe pumps that took her barely five-and-a-half feet to five nine or so. Plus she'd gone and gotten a fabulous pedicure, and she wanted to show off the bright red polish she had on.

"What? Just because I can dig a bullet from downed shifters and shoot a gun doesn't mean I don't like high heels." She did, in fact. She had more pairs of shoes than she should have, but she didn't feel bad about it. As addictions went, it wasn't a bad one.

"I'm glad you do." He held out an arm and she took it.

"You look very handsome." He really did. She hadn't seen him dressed up before. The black tie against the black suit should have been odd, but wasn't. He'd tied his hair back, exposing more of his face. Ridiculously gorgeous.

"I do?"

She buckled in and he walked around to his side.

"Yes."

"Can't be as beautiful as you look. You've got legs made for skirts."

She blushed. "Thanks."

"I wanted to let you know we're still working on the shooting situation. They've removed the old Alpha and several other members from their jamboree ranks."

"Wow. Really? I mean, good, they should. But to remove an Alpha, that's complicated I imagine."

He was quiet a while before he answered, which wasn't totally unusual, he was a man of very few words. But this felt different.

"Each jamboree handles it in their own way, but yes, it's complicated to replace any cats from leadership positions in a jamboree. To unseat an Alpha and a Bringer will be a great upheaval for Smithville. If those fuckers hadn't shot me and you, I'd probably feel worse about it."

"I don't feel bad when people act like thugs and have to pay a price. All for what? Getting pissy because they brought too many cats into your territory and got slapped? It's not like dominance games aren't part and parcel of our world."

"The price will be paid by the other cats in the jamboree. That's what I feel bad about."

Beneath that grumpy, broody male exterior, there was a big giant heart. He pretended like he was hard all the time, but she saw through that. Saw through the Bringer he wore like a second skin to the compassion and gentleness beneath.

She knew he'd be uncomfortable if she commented on that so she poked at him instead. A girl had to keep him on his toes, clearly.

"Yes, I'm aware of how the things leaders of the jamboree do hurt others."

He snorted. "Back on that? I hear your grandmother had coffee with my mother."

"Apparently she's still alive. I didn't see anything in the paper. I'd count that as a success. That and your mother called to remind me about tonight. Twice."

He may have quirked up a grin. He was unreadable sometimes.

"She respects your grandmother. She can be hard to win over."

"My grandmother?"

He laughed then. "I meant my mother, but from what I've heard and how you are, I'd imagine that extends to her as well."

"I'm not hard to win over."

"Ha."

"Ha? Is that the best you've got? Ha?"

"You're stubborn. And temperamental."

"I'm resolute and in touch with my emotions." She tried to sound haughty, but in her attempt not to laugh it didn't come off as good as she'd have liked.

"Ha."

"So anyway, what's the plan for tonight? I don't have to give a speech or anything? Your mother was less than forthcoming."

"She likes to keep people on their toes. But as far as I know, it's just a dinner. My brother Max will make a speech of some kind. He's a speech type of guy. He's grateful for your service and not totally unaware of the history between our families."

"We've been to jamboree events, you know. Every year we do the children's hospital picnic. We answer the call when it's made."

"I can't believe I've never noticed you at any of the gatherings."

"There are too many people there to notice, I'd wager. We kept to ourselves and our small group. You were probably prowling around being scary anyway."

"I'm sorry."

She was reaching out to touch his hand before she'd even realized she was doing it. She brushed her fingertips over the back of his fingers, over his knuckles. "It's not on you. And it's old history, as you point out. I made the joke at the end, you know, to soften it."

But he kept serious. "The jamboree is a source of great comfort to me. Safety. Loyalty. I'm sorry it wasn't that for you and I hope things change. It shouldn't have been a place of dread. Our job as the governing family is to open our doors and care for our cats. We haven't done that with your family. I regret that."

"Did you do it personally? Repeat lies about my grandmother?"

"No, and I understand what you're saying. But it's something we'd like to remedy. Not the lies, we can't undo the past. But this is your jamboree. I...we want you to be at home within it."

She gave in and smiled. "Thank you."

She didn't know why he was so anxious when they arrived. He went to get her door and for once she allowed it. That flustered him. Her hand in his as he helped her down was warm, and he kept it as they headed toward the house.

Chapter Seven

"Gibson, come in!" A pretty woman opened the door.

Mia froze a moment. The other woman's scent was cat, yes, but something else too.

"Mia Porter, this is Kendra de La Vega. She's Max's wife."

"And my Alpha." And a witch, which is why she had that difference in scent. Mia dipped her head just enough. There was no call to be rude, after all. But she didn't need to give her obeisance to this female just yet.

Kendra took her hands. "It's really my pleasure to meet you. I like Gibson in one piece, you see. And you saved him. Thank you. Please come in and out to the backyard. Imogene is out there ordering people around and making it look like she's only suggesting things."

Mia couldn't help but like Kendra, with her dry humor and easy affection toward her brother-in-law.

"Is my father around? I'd like to have him meet Mia before everyone arrives."

A tall, beautiful man throwing off so much testosterone it was clear he was Gibson's big brother, Max, came down the hall as they entered the main part of the house. "Mia Porter, I presume?"

Suddenly shy, she nodded. Gibson squeezed the hand he still held, and she found her courage again. "Yes, and you must be Max." She averted her eyes a moment as she tipped her chin down.

"I am. And I'm very pleased to meet you in person so I can thank you for your service to our jamboree. Gibson has told us about the shooting and the situation with the car chase the other night. Though he's often gruff, we like having him around."

Gibson snorted and she relaxed a little.

She'd accepted thanks enough on this that she had gotten past her initial tendency to blow it off. As her grandmother had told her, it was important to let people thank you and important to be gracious in response.

"You're welcome. Thank you for having me here this evening."

Max's smile went from all business to something more relaxed. "My mother loves to have parties. It's nice to give her a good reason."

Kendra came back to their group and Max pulled her to his side. "She hasn't even made it outside yet, boys." She turned her attention back to Mia. "Would you like a drink? There's a full bar set up out back." Their metabolisms were too fast to really get drunk, but a nice glass of wine was good for you—an adage her father repeated often.

"Sure, that would be lovely." She turned back to Gibson. "I've met your father. Once, a long time ago." She'd seen them all from afar as she'd grown up.

"I hadn't thought of that. Of course. But he'd still like to speak to you." He leaned in closer. "You'll like him. Nearly everyone does."

The backyard was set up for dinner. Several long tables were topped with pretty place settings and flickering candles. She envied them this huge outdoor space. Children ran and played off to the side of the main yard. Fenced and full of things for them to run and jump all over. It made her smile. The surreptitious guard posted didn't make her so gooey inside, but she knew the reason for it and was glad their young were all safe.

"My nieces and nephews."

She heartily approved of the way it appeared the de La Vegas cared for their young. Family was the most important thing.

Gibson liked the way she smiled as she caught sight of the kids. She was nearly shy, which he had imagined he'd find annoying given her general fearlessness, but instead he was touched by it.

"Ah! You're here." His mother, her expression lightening when she caught sight of them, paused to take some drinks from a tray before continuing on her way over, Cesar, his father, at her side.

"Mia Porter, thank you for your service to this jamboree and to my son. I am in your debt." Cesar bowed deeply to Mia, who blinked, wide eyed at his father's old-school chivalry.

"I...thank you. Even if he was a de La Vega." She smiled to underline that it was a joke.

Cesar took her hands, laughing. "A sense of humor is most welcome. As are you. We're happy to have you here."

Imogene handed Mia a glass. "Champagne?"

Mia, now freed from his father's grip, took the glass. "Yes, thank you."

"Gibson, show her around. Introduce her. Oh and thank you for your recommendation. We have a case of the borsao from your shop. Cesar loves red wine."

"And good Spanish red as well."

His father grinned back, flirting now. "Indeed. We love wine and food."

"It's one of my favorite things about the Spanish."

Gibson liked this side of her. The ease she had with his father warmed him. Imogene sent him a look and he knew she was thinking the same. Admittedly he was relieved. Things had most decidedly not been easy between Renee and Imogene when Galen first brought her around.

It was better now. In fact his sister-in-law and his mother were very close. But he'd have hated it if there had been tension.

Of course because he wanted the Porters back in the jamboree and he knew it was important for them all to be united in the face of all the chaos just outside.

He held his arm out and she took it. "I'm ready for my tour."

She didn't look too overwhelmed. In fact, she'd warmed up as they strolled around the yard and he introduced her. Several people already knew her, which he was glad of. Not so much the way a few of the males took her in, their gazes lingering on those legs he'd complimented earlier. He kept a hand at the small of her back, knowing he shouldn't but not stopping himself. She wasn't his, but she sure as hell wasn't going to be anyone else's. Not then anyway.

"Ah, there are my parents. Come on. You haven't met them yet and I've been ordered to introduce you." She waved to the cats who'd come out to the yard from the house. He'd seen pictures of course. He did look into her and her family after the first night. But it was so clear they adored her. He liked to see it.

"Mom, Dad, Grandma, this is Gibson de La Vega. Gibson, this is my mother Ellen, my father Jim and my grandmother Lettie."

He nodded to the father and then the mother and bent over the grandmother's hand. Lettie fluttered her lashes and flirted with him, nearly making him smile. He could see where Mia got her spine though when she straightened and gave the area a once-over.

"Last time I was here...well, never mind that."

Mia kissed Lettie's cheek and spoke in her ear. Gibson could have tuned it out. Because of super-sensitive shifter hearing, many times they had to force their attention away from a whispered conversation for courtesy's sake. But he wasn't feeling courteous, he was curious.

"If you're uncomfortable, we can go right now."

Lettie held her granddaughter's gaze. "You're a good girl. I'm fine. I still have sharp claws if anyone comes at me."

He had to bite the inside of his cheek at that. He just bet she did.

Drew came out with his girlfriend, a cat whose family was quite active in jamboree events. And Dario's sister. She waved in their direction and dragged Drew over. "Hello." She hugged Mia. "My dad wanted me to tell you there's going to be an apartment coming up available in my building. In two months."

Mia's expression brightened. "Really? Thanks for the head's up. I'll check in next week."

He hadn't known she was looking for a place. He'd have to follow up on that with her later on.

Lauren Dane

His sister Beth came out, holding his newest nephew. She'd had a rough time with both Kendra and Renee when they'd come into the jamboree. Her insecurity and resentment had made a once really wonderful and fun person into one weighted down with bitterness and a special sort of hate for humans. He didn't know what to expect from her that night, but he hoped the baby would keep her calm.

He had to admit she was better, even just a little bit, in the wake of the horrible betrayal of their brother Carlos, who'd been working with the human anti-Other hate groups. That had shocked them all and had been a powerful—and painful—reminder of what was important.

Their mother moved to Beth, cooing and then snatching the baby from Beth's arms. Few people loved babies more than Imogene. Beth smiled at their mother, shaking her head. He ached for the person his sister used to be.

"Dinner is about to start." Cesar came out into the back. "Take your seats if you please. Gibson, please bring Mia and her family up here." He indicated the table where the governing cats would sit.

"Ooh. Special." She whispered it and he squeezed her hand, which he'd found himself holding an awful lot that evening.

"Don't forget it, missy."

His mother had spared no effort to make the evening lovely. The food was delicious, the drinks flowed and the chatter all around was easy and upbeat. It had been a while since it had been so drama free.

Max had given a speech. A warm, brief one that thanked Mia and her family. In his way he underlined how delighted they were to have the Porters there but managed to do it in a way that wouldn't put anyone on the spot. There was a reason his brother was such a good Alpha.

At last he sat down, and everyone relaxed again and got back to eating and talking.

"So I'm told you were in the military. What did you do?"

Mia looked up from her plate to listen to Max's question.

Instead, it was her mother who answered. "Mia's a pilot. An amazing one. And she was decorated several times for bravery while she was in Iraq."

Gibson hid a smile. Her mother was an awful lot like his. Clearly proud of her kids.

"Really?" Max flicked his gaze from Ellen back to Mia. "I don't think I'm surprised given what Gibson has told me. What are you going to do now?"

"I don't really know yet. I'm working on that."

"Is it hard to get work as a pilot? Or are you wanting to do other things?" Kendra put another pork chop on Max's plate before she added one to her own. Gibson loved the way she took care of Max. And truth be told, was a little envious.

"As you might be aware, Weres have been fired and barred from working for some airlines. Mainly I flew C130s and other large cargo planes. A challenge, but I enjoyed it." Her lips flattened for a moment, and he wondered, yet again, what the hell had happened to her.

"Just give it time." Drew spoke softly. But of course everyone heard and their nosiness took over.

"Did something happen? Were you injured in Iraq?" Renee asked.

"Renee is a healer. It's her magickal gift." Galen leaned over and kissed his wife's temple.

"I was injured in Iraq, yes."

"Twice," Ellen added.

"Thanks, Mom." She sent her mother a look, but it was Lettie who made a dismissive sound.

"She's ashamed of her attack. As if it was her fault."

"Grandma, that's enough." She vibrated with tension, and while he desperately wanted to hear the rest, Mia was clearly upset and didn't want to talk about it. He found himself rubbing a hand up and down her back. And her father sent him a raised brow.

But he didn't stop.

"So, you have another son?" Kendra smoothly interceded, asking Ellen.

Lettie wasn't done. "She was attacked, pulled off the street in Los Angeles. Two miles from her apartment. They beat her up. Nearly killed her. Used silver on her. Silver-tipped hammer they said."

Mia went totally white and Gibson's stomach clenched.

She stood. "Please excuse me." Her normally easy posture was stiff and ramrod straight.

"Stop it," Jim said to Lettie quietly. Ellen looked to Mia, anxiety on her face. Imogene met her son's eyes, clearly worried.

Lettie rapped the table with her knuckles. "She hides it like it's her fault. It's not her fault. She has no call to be ashamed. I know a few things about that. I won't have her feeling guilty about other people's crimes."

Gibson stood as well. "Hey, let's all just calm down. You don't have to talk about anything you don't want to talk about." He kept Mia's gaze, nearly losing his shit when he caught sight of the tears threatening to overflow. "Would you like to see the garden? It's just over there. Has a great view."

She nodded woodenly and let him lead her from the table.

The chatter, which had come to a screeching halt, began again. Stilted at first, but it picked up again as they continued to move away from the tables and toward the garden his father loved so much.

"I can take you home if you like. But no one wants that." He opened the gate his father had installed to keep animals and toddlers away from his garden.

She went in and paused to take in the space all around her. "This is unexpected."

Like she was to him. "My father has a gift. Living things respond to him." He tipped his head to a bench that was out of sight of the rest of the gathering.

She sat and he joined her, pulling her close, and she didn't stop him.

"Do you want to talk about it? Just between us?"

"I survived two tours in Iraq. People tried to kill me all the time." She snorted. "It became part of the background noise, all that danger. It began to seem normal, the amount of time and effort it took simply to leave each day. I got back and I wasn't ready to come home. Back to Boston I mean. I landed in LA with a friend I'd been in the Air Force with. We shared an apartment. She found a job pretty quickly. I'd been offered a job teaching at a flight school." She shrugged. "I was mulling it over and living off my savings."

Things got quiet for a while. The hum of conversation and the clinking of glasses and flatware in the background.

"Lots of Others in LA, you know. But it's different there. Infighting. There are so many people from so many places. It's exciting and sort of scary all at once. And the humans, the anti-Others I mean, they're active. So I was already pretty conscious of myself and my surroundings when I went out. It was daylight. Like one-in-the-afternoon daylight. I'd been at lunch, working a shift for another friend for something to do and a little extra cash. On the way back to my car there was this group of men. Humans. But I'm a fucking jaguar, you know? Christ, I turn furry and have sharp claws! I thought I could handle anything."

How stupid she'd been.

"But as I walked to skirt around them, ignoring their taunts, one of them hit me in the back of the head, and when I stumbled, they yanked me into the building behind them. An old warehouse of some sort."

She could still smell the abandoned space. The dust and mold. The leather of their shoes and the stink of sweat and fear. And hate.

"They all just started hitting me and I wanted to change, but then someone *stabbed* me. In the side." She touched the spot absently. At that moment she'd thought, outraged, that they'd actually stabbed her. And then she realized why she wasn't shifting. "It was silver and I couldn't change. And there were so many. All hitting." She'd tried very hard to keep her feet, knowing if she fell that'd be the end.

He growled low in his throat, but otherwise kept silent.

"Then they started using other things to hurt me. I used my right arm, my right side to try to fend them off. Anyway, I don't remember exactly what they used after that. Only that they tore into the muscle and flesh of my chest and shoulder, and it hurt so bad. So bad my cat went mad, wanting to change. I'd never felt anything like it before. I lost consciousness. They hit me in the head again a few times."

She moved a little and he put an arm around her shoulder. She shivered, but not from the cold. Tears thickened her voice, and she was so tired, so relieved to just be telling the story that she didn't care.

"Some women had been working across the street and had seen them pull me into the building. They called the cops. They saved my life. I'd bled so much I would have died from that if the silver they sprinkled into the open wounds on my chest hadn't poisoned me first. One of the cops was a werewolf. Thank God. He kept the questions about what I was to a minimum. They assumed I was a werewolf like him. I lived." She took a deep breath and let herself hear that. "I fucking lived, Gibson. They didn't want me to, but I'm alive and I won't forget."

He shook. No matter how hard he tried not to shake, he still shook. The catch in her voice and the way her heart sped up when she told him the story, the subtle scent of her fear and shame, it all battered him.

This fucking hate was ugly. What drove people to such behavior?

"What happened to them?"

"My attackers? They ran when the cops arrived. They sort of tried to find them. I'm being unfair. The overwhelming percentage of people I dealt with in the hospital and with the cops were good to me. They wanted to help. Wanted me to survive. Wanted to find the fuckers who'd hurt me. But not all of them and the ones who didn't care are why, I believe, no arrests have been made."

"Was there lasting damage?"

She nodded, her gaze glassy as she stared out over the garden. "I was in a coma for a week."

For a shifter to be out that long meant she'd been so close to death her system shut down to continue to operate at the most minimal level until her body could heal.

"As for the rest? The silver filings they used in the open wounds in my shoulder fucked up my muscles. Some of the damage is permanent. At first I couldn't even use my right arm. I've been going to physical therapy. I've gotten a great deal of my strength back, but if I'm lucky I'll be at eighty percent. I used to rock climb. They don't advise it now. And my coordination has been affected as well."

"Can you fly anymore?"

"A lot of flying these days is really done with computers and autopilot. So I can do that, easily. And I'm told I can fly smaller aircraft and helicopters again once I get the okay from my PT. I don't know about the other stuff, the speed of response and all that jazz."

He heaved a sigh. "Christ. I'm sorry. Not sorry you can fly still. Because that's a good thing."

"Hopefully anyway."

"If anyone can do it, you can."

"We'll see. I have about eighty percent of an engineering degree. I've been toying with going back."

"Do you want to be an engineer?"

She laughed. "Not really."

"Do you want to fly again?"

"I love to fly."

"What's stopping you? If you can fly helicopters and smaller planes, that is."

"I don't know."

"Yes you do."

"I wish we could get drunk."

Surprised, he laughed. "Renee has this potion she makes. It started as a way to put Weres under for surgery. But it's really moonshine. I didn't make that up. My brother Galen calls it hooch."

"Maybe later." She sighed and he kissed the top of her head.

"I hear sex is also a good relaxer and mood enhancer."

She laughed and he let some of his tension go. "That so?"

"It's what I hear." He paused a while. "You favor your left side sometimes. Is that weakness or are you in pain?"

She shifted, looking down at her hands. "Both. The doctors don't really have a lot of experience with the lasting effects of silver poisoning. But it's a possibility that the chronic pain will be permanent."

He pushed to stand, needing the room to stalk a little. His cat was so very close, his control so very thin.

"But that day, the day I got shot, you lugged me to your apartment."

"I'm not totally weak. I'm still a shifter."

He loved the way she jutted her chin out. Defiant.

"I'm getting better. Three weeks ago I could barely stand. I couldn't use my right hand at all. I had to go to physical therapy three times a week. Now I'm down to once a week. I'm so much stronger than I was."

"Your grandmother is proud of you. And she's right, you shouldn't feel guilty about what other people have done. This attack wasn't your fault."

"Be that as it may, she has no right to share that with a whole room of strangers. No one needs to know unless I decide to tell them. It changes how people look at you. I don't have time for that."

He understood. In ways he'd never be able to put into words. Understood what it meant to always look strong in the presence of others. Especially other cats.

"She's an elder. And your grandmother. As far as I can see she's not shy either."

That made her laugh.

Chapter Eight

When they got back to his car, after she'd been talked to by what seemed like a thousand people and her mother had apologized for her grandmother, and she'd told her mother it wasn't necessary, Gibson had asked her to hold on a moment because he had to speak with Dario about something.

Once he'd moved off, her father approached. "I'm sorry. She loves you, you know. She wanted everyone there to understand how amazing you are."

Mia nodded. "Don't apologize for her. She'll only be mad at you if she finds out. It's who she is. I get it. She didn't mean to hurt me. I know."

He hugged her. "I'm proud of you. We're all proud of you. This was supposed to be your night."

She laughed then. "Dad, it's all right. I promise. She can't be anyone other than who she is. And now it's not a secret and that's all right too, I suppose. Anyway, it was a nice dinner, and I'm full and glad things appear to be on the mend between us and the de La Vegas."

"What's Gibson to you then?"

"What?"

"Honey, are you really going to play that game with your father? Don't waste my time. I watched him all night. He comforted you and you responded. He shielded you every time you two stood near each other."

"It's nothing serious. He's investigating... Oh hell, I don't know." She snorted. "Really I don't. But it's not an engagement. He's not a jerk. I'm not a jerk. We enjoy each other's company."

"If I thought he was a jerk, I'd have never come here tonight. But don't fool yourself into thinking the way you two are is anything less than the seeds of imprinting. And if you go that route, you'd better understand what it is to be with a male like him. You grew up with laid-back men. Gibson is *not* laid-back. He's an alpha."

Boy did she know that.

"I'm not imprinting. I can have a relationship with another cat without it being imprinting."

Jaguar shifters didn't mate for life in the same way wolves did. There was no one true mate binding of DNA. But what they did was imprint. Their cats settled in, got the scent of the other, marked their territory. And once a cat did that, once the human allowed it and let themselves imprint on the other person and that other cat with them, it was forever. Forever in the same way the wolves had.

Cats could get married without imprinting. Many did. But Gibson de La Vega wasn't the type of male who'd settle down without being imprinted. His cat wouldn't submit to anyone else who wasn't his forever. It was an important reminder of who she was dallying with. But she couldn't lie and pretend the idea of imprinting wasn't important to her as well. Her parents were imprinted. She wanted that connection with someone.

But for the time being, they were just enjoying each other. And that was that.

"You can fool yourself, baby girl. But you can't fool your daddy." He kissed her forehead, and she rubbed her cheek along his jawline as she hugged him.

"Go on home. I'll see you tomorrow."

Her grandmother stalked right up and put her hands on her hips. "I am not sorry these other cats know what an impressive woman you are."

She held back a smile, nodding. "Grandma, I love you. I understand why you did it. But that was what happened to me. It was my story to tell. Or not."

"I never want you to feel guilty for anyone else's crimes. I *know* what it is to feel that sort of estrangement. You don't deserve that. To be alone and misunderstood. I won't have it."

She was going to make Mia cry, damn it.

Mia hugged her grandmother before Lettie went back to the car where her father waited.

Gibson approached moments later. "Everything all right?"

She took a deep breath. "Yeah. It's fine."

"Good. I think you should come over to my place."

She allowed that smile at last. "Yeah? Are you going to sully me?"

"At least twice and I don't want to do it in your brother's bed."

She laughed and let him open her door. "Let's go, then."

She liked to watch the city roll by out her window as he drove. He was a man of few words. There was quiet between them, but it wasn't strained. She didn't feel the need to fill it with chatter, or to feel as if he didn't care. He just didn't speak unless it was very important.

And it gave her a chance to think about what her father had said. Because Gibson *had* shielded her. He'd stroked a hand up and down her back when she'd been alarmed. He'd sat with her, arm around her shoulder as she poured out the horror of that day back in Los Angeles. It was...well, she...it made her a little tingly.

He was big and bad and totally in charge, but he didn't take over. That was a plus. And he was an adult, which meant, contrary to what her father said, he could have this thing with her and not imprint or be bossy or whatever. Neither of them were strangers to having a relationship, though she got the feeling his long-term relationships were all with his family and not romantic ones. But there was no reason for it to be anything more than some great times in bed and getting to know each other.

She turned her head to look at him. His face intent as he drove. In profile he was even more impressive than straight on. His features were so strong, so handsome and slightly feral. There was no mistaking that this was one hundred percent male. He wore a tie and his hair back, and he looked damned fine. But you could shine up the outside and it did not change the fact that he was a brawler. A predator who would bust heads to protect his own.

It made her smile.

He hit the garage door opener, and out of the dark, two cats seemed to melt into existence. His place was well guarded, she knew. The cats averted their eyes when he got out, and she waited for him to open her side. He spoke to them briefly, and they melted into the darkness again as he'd made his way to her door.

He'd been so sweet to her that evening, and she knew it made him happy to do things like open her door and pull out her chair so she let him. Usually.

He smiled as she took his hand and got down. It was not as easy in four-and-a-half-inch heels as it was in her sneakers or boots, and the damned SUV was so high up she needed his help to get down anyway. But then he grabbed her around her waist and she slid down his body until her mouth was at his, staying her to take a kiss. He took a slow, meandering taste of her as he backed her against the car.

All she could do was sigh and hold on as his mouth was on hers. He kissed with the same intensity he did everything else. A nip of her lip, a quick flutter of his tongue against hers, he used his lips, teeth and tongue to render her witless and full of his taste.

When he finally eased her to her feet, she had to gulp in some air before she could put her thoughts and muscles together enough to walk with him into his house.

His house had been a surprise the first time she'd been there the night she'd been shot and had cleaned the glass from his shoulder. It was masculine with clean lines—that wasn't so unusual. That fit him quite well. But the reading nook he'd built into the bay window in his bedroom had been an unexpected delight. Books were everywhere, shelves lined his walls. Big, overstuffed chairs presented lots of opportunities to sit and read the day away. Though she figured he probably didn't get as much of that kind of time as he'd like.

There was a sense of home and comfort there he'd built and was proud of.

"You should keep the shoes on." He led her up the stairs toward his bedroom.

"Should I?"

"I have to tell you it's a recurring fantasy of mine to fuck you while you're in heels. Well since I saw you in them and now I can't stop thinking of it. It's been in my head all night long."

She tossed her bag on the small bench at the foot of his rather ridiculously large bed. "I think I can be about some wish fulfillment." She undid her hair, which she'd had up in a loose bun and then unbuttoned the front of her blouse.

He stepped close and bent his head to her chest, his lips brushing over the swell of her right breast. "You smell damned good. Makes me hungry." He licked over the skin and goose bumps rose. "You know how much I like to eat you up."

She swallowed, hard, still not used to how sexy he was when he said stuff like that. He was in charge of his sexuality. He told her what he liked, what he wanted and that was unbelievably hot. Especially when he didn't say much outside the bedroom.

"Not gonna argue."

He popped the catch on her bra and pushed it and her blouse from her body.

He kissed her chest and over her scars. That gentle touch so intimate tears sprang to her eyes. He'd done it before, yes, but now he knew the details of the story and he hadn't shrunk away. He hadn't been repulsed.

Big hands cupped her breasts and then his fingers went to work, pinching and tugging her nipples until she moaned and grabbed the waist of his pants, yanking to get them open.

"You're very demanding and impatient." He kissed up her neck to her ear to that spot he knew drove her insane. And it did, making her knees buckle.

He nipped the spot, bringing a hiss to her lips as she struggled to push him back to finish getting his pants open.

"You promised to sully me. You're the Bringer, you're supposed to keep your word. Get your dick out!"

He laughed, picking her up and tossing her on his bed. She watched every move as he took off his shirt and tie.

"Your body makes me sort of dizzy."

He paused, his hands on his pants, slowly unzipping. "Says the topless woman in my bed." He finished, stepping from his pants.

"You have no underpants on!" She laughed and then unzipped her skirt. "Me either."

He jumped to the bed, so graceful and full of power it left her breathless.

"You're so dirty. God, I love that. How you could be so totally filthy and yet look so sweet on the outside, it undoes me."

Mia pressed her face to his neck, licking the salt of his skin. "Take your hair down. I love it down."

He reached back one-handed to undo his hair while the other tossed the now-discarded skirt to the side.

He hadn't lied, she totally undid him. Her skin, the way she moved, the way she was so open and greedy about sex, her fearlessness, all of it made her into the total package and it drove him to his knees.

She made him laugh in bed. It had been years since that had happened.

He grunted when she grabbed his cock while she licked up his neck. Half a foot shorter than he was and she held her own, writhing against him as he slid a palm down her belly to find her pussy wet and inferno hot. She rolled her hips and urged him on with a whispered *more*.

But then she scissored her legs and maneuvered up, getting him on his back as she straddled his body.

"Were you on the wrestling team, baby?"

Her smile was a mystery as she dipped down to capture his mouth, as she held him close, tugging on his dreads to get him where she wanted. Her taste was glory. Beauty and seduction. She nibbled his bottom lip.

"I love your mouth. This lip here." She licked over it as she scooted down a little. "So full and plump. Mmmm." Down again as she kissed his throat and to each nipple. She licked and sucked, tugging on each ring until he growled at her for more. Again that smile of hers.

She kissed over his belly. Over the de La Vega inked there, dipping her tongue into his navel, making him shiver a moment. She kissed his hip and the shallow, sensitive spot at the hollow of his hipbone. And then she grabbed his cock, angling it as she brought her gaze to his. "This." She hummed her delight.

Before he could say anything she licked across the head and around the crown before taking him into her mouth totally. She palmed his sac as she kept sucking, keeping it tight and very wet. Leaving her gaze on him.

So. Fucking. Intimate. He wanted to look away. She got inside him and he wasn't entirely comfortable with it. But his cat seemed to claw his guts at the very idea. His cat loved this boldness in a female, just as much as the man loved the hell out of his cock in her mouth.

He held his control in check, not wanting to gag her. She pulled off and licked her lips. "Let go."

He shook his head. "I'm fine. Don't stop!"

She shook her head right back. "I can feel your muscles trembling. What is it you want? Hm?" As she said it, she slid her fingertips back to stroke over his asshole and he groaned.

"Hadn't thought of that." He nearly panted.

"Then what?"

"I want to fuck your mouth."

"So why don't you?"

She sucked him into her mouth again and her fingertips found his asshole once more, this time slick with lube she'd gathered from her pussy.

The air came from him like a punch. So fucking good he didn't want to stop so he rolled his hips, and she adjusted herself to take him in easier as he widened his thighs to give her better access.

He couldn't have stopped unless she'd ordered him to. And she most assuredly did not as he continued to stroke into that sweet mouth. And when a finger breached that first ring of muscle, the burn made him pause until it spread into a heat that was far more pleasure than pain.

She worked, mouth in concert with the questing, inexorable invasion of his ass, and when she found his sweet spot and began to rub it, he nearly lost his mind and blew down her throat right then.

So good, it was a challenge to make it another three minutes until he came with a snarl of her name.

He lay there, struggling to get his breath back as the reason for it snuggled up into his side. Naked except for those sexy fucking heels.

"Don't go anywhere, you're next."

She smiled, her mouth against his skin.

"Now that my lips and teeth aren't numb, come a little closer."

She levered up, leaning on his chest, and he lazily slid his fingertips down the line of her spine. So feminine, even as she could shoot and punch and curse with the best of them.

"Why don't you climb aboard?" He sent her a raised brow.

She blushed and he turned to his side to kiss her better. "Why you blushing? Hm? Not that I'm complaining, your scent when you blush gets lush and sexy."

"I haven't done it that way."

"You've never had your pussy eaten while you sit on your man's face?" He wasn't much of a dirty talker, but she drove him to it. With her the limits seemed silly. With her it was all out there, whether he wanted it to be or not.

She shook her head. "Nope."

"Mmm, well let's go step by step. I know you know how to get on top."

She sat up, slinging a leg over his waist. She rubbed her pussy over his quickly reviving cock, and he sucked in a breath. "Stop that. I can't concentrate."

She grinned. "Yeah?"

He grabbed her hips to hold her still. "Yeah. So scoot up here." He urged her, his hands still at her hips. "Hands on the headboard so you can keep your balance, and then put that sweet cunt over my mouth and I'll do the rest."

She moved that last little bit as he caressed up her thighs, holding her open. The only sad thing was that he couldn't see her face, but her taste was on his lips, against his tongue as the slickness of her pussy was all he wanted to know.

Her muscles trembled and he thought about her thigh a moment. It had healed, but he didn't want her to be in pain. But she made a sound, a low, desperate sound that told him her claws might come unsheathed if he didn't get back to work right then.

She'd never been so exposed. It wasn't just that she...that he was there beneath her, his mouth on her. He'd done that before and she was more than pleased with his skills. It was that she was above him this way, that she found her fingers tightening on the headboard to keep from grabbing him by the hair and yanking him up to get more. She'd told him about her attack and he'd understood. He'd seen her cry. There seemed to be no way to hide from him. Not sexually and not emotionally. It was exhilarating and terrifying at the same time.

He sucked her clit into his mouth over and over, slowly. His hands, so big and strong, were spread over the backs of her thighs, holding her legs apart as he nuzzled and licked her pussy until she thought she'd scream from how good it felt.

She closed her eyes and let it go. Why be embarrassed by this when she'd had his cock in her mouth and her finger in his ass just minutes before? There was nowhere to hide when it came to sex between them, she realized and then accepted.

Which was a good thing because she found herself unable to stop rolling her hips to stroke herself against his mouth. His answering growl echoed up her body, letting her know he was just fine with it, even more, he dug it. His whiskers—which she knew he used conditioner on to keep soft—brushed against her inner thighs and when he opened his mouth against her, his tongue sliding over every part of her pussy, she let her head drop forward as orgasm hit her so hard her entire body trembled from it.

But he kept going. Even as she moved to sit back, he kept her there, driving her past that nearly painful oversensitivity and into another orgasm until at last he laid her back on the bed.

She cracked an eye to find that smug smile on his lips. "How'd that go?"

She laughed. "You aced the finals."

She really couldn't believe she was jogging. She hated jogging. But her physical therapist had suggested it as another way to build endurance so she was doing it, and sweating like a pig shifter.

That made her laugh, which was good because it meant she had enough breath not to pass out. She kept running, glad for all the paths around town so she could keep up some variety. She had an audiobook in her iPod but for right then she'd switched to Florence + the Machine. Each drumbeat kept her feet pounding the pavement. Her thigh had mostly healed and she thanked her shifter blood for that. But it had been slower going than it would have been before the attack.

She picked up her pace and ignored the twinges. It was unacceptable that she not be back to one hundred percent. Unacceptable that those assholes who'd nearly killed her might limit her choices any more than they already had.

Her shoes connected with the path, boom, boom, boom, like her heart. The rhythm lulling her.

Up the trail she kept track of the people on bikes coming in the opposite direction and got over, not wanting to cause a crash. *Boom, boom, boom.* She kept running, but they kept edging into her space until she realized it wasn't just drift, but purposeful.

The cottony place she'd been in as she ran fell away. Her senses sharpened as she took everything all around her in. How fast they moved, the looks on their faces, the lack of others on the trail.

And despite her training, despite the fact that she'd been under threat and was on the lookout for anything out of the ordinary, it was still unreal.

Like an ugly dream as reality pulled away from her shores and she watched as a weapon was pulled and aimed in her direction. She hit the ground and rolled to the right, toward a stand of bushes that would hopefully give her some cover.

They tossed the bikes and headed toward her. She pulled her phone out and called Gibson and got out her location and that she was being attacked and was going to shift. She hung up and let her cat come over, let the anger and rage spill into her, speeding the full transformation until she bounded from the bushes and ran toward the two men with guns. Only they weren't men, they were cats.

Cats that weren't nearly as brave and they tried to run. Her cat didn't take too kindly to that, and she landed on one of them as he was in mid-shift. The other behind her shot but it missed her as she snarled and then hissed.

She ripped at the one beneath her, her cat no longer afraid, but full-on pissed off.

Someone was on her back. She twisted, her claws out, shredding the other cat until it shrieked and tried to get away. She grabbed it with her teeth, needing to kill before she ended up dead. Her cat remembering the helplessness of the last time. Remembering what it was to be nearly killed.

Sadly for those two who tried to harm her.

But human voices came down the trail. And then sirens. The woman inside insisted the cat move on and get out of sight. The cat reluctantly left her bleeding prey and bounded off toward home.

Gibson saw it was her number and, smiling, he answered. But instead of her normal voice, she was upset. Tense. She spoke quickly and quietly. "Two men on bikes with weapons. They're following me. I'm shifting." She dropped the phone and he heard the sound of her cat's scream. His own rushed to the surface, his hands fisting against phantom claws.

He grabbed his keys, standing, though he'd been involved in a meeting. Several sets of eyes looked his way. "Mia is being attacked again. Dario, with me."

Dario took the wheel as Gibson watched out the window. He kept his phone to his ear but the call was dropped. But not before he heard the attack, the sound of teeth meeting flesh, and he hoped like hell it was her cat who was ripping those others apart.

He knew where the trail was. He'd been the one to suggest it to her because it wasn't so often used by others, and she hated to run where it was crowded.

But cop cars were there when they arrived. Dario put his hand out to stay him. "I know you're worried, but you can't do anything with the cops there."

Ambulances had pulled up. "Fuck that. What if she's hurt?"

"What can you do for her if she is? You're not married to her. You can't ride in the ambulance with her. They're going to want to know who you are. How can you explain it?"

"I'm not going to sit here watching as she dies. What kind of cat do you think I am?" He pushed from the car but walked around the scene, using his nose to find the spot where she'd hit the bushes. Her phone was there, along with her clothes. He grabbed them and climbed down the small hillside to the street below. It was only about a mile to her apartment so he headed that way, calling Dario to tell him to meet him a few blocks away.

"I'm not saying you don't care about her. I'm saying be smart." Dario risked continuing the conversation when he got back into the car.

"She's one of my cats. Do you think I'd walk away if it was you? Or her brother or any of my people? It's my job. I am the Bringer. It is my role to keep her and others like her, safe."

"I'm sure it has nothing to do with the fact that you're falling in love with her."

He glared but Dario had known him long enough to let that go.

Once they'd arrived at the stoplight a block away from her building he got out and headed over. "Meet me there."

He didn't bother with calling up. The door was being opened by someone leaving and he caught it, heading up to her place via the stairs. He pounded on the door. "Mia, are you in there?"

She opened moments later, holding a towel over herself.

He pushed inside and locked up. "What's going on?" He took the towel, ignoring her squawk of annoyance, and gave her a close look. She stopped struggling, and he was so angry that anyone would touch her that he could ignore all that pretty skin he usually wanted to lick from head to toe.

"I'm all right. Mainly. One of them tore at my back. That'll take another hour or so. They fucking shot at me. *Shot at me!* What the hell? They were shifters. The same scent as the night you were shot. I don't think they used silver though."

"Get your things." He stalked, pacing back and forth.

"What? I'm not going to the hospital. I was attacked when I was shifted. Those fuckers were not anywhere near as good as me."

"Don't try to be cute."

"I don't have to try. Don't hate, Gibson. I'm naturally cute. Why are you all Pacy McPacerson over there?"

"What if they know where you live? You can stay with me. Or with your parents. Or with my parents for that matter. You're one of our cats."

Her eyes widened, and he realized he'd made some sort of man mistake but didn't know what it was.

"You look here. I am no one's responsibility. You got me?"

"What? Of course you are. They clearly think you saw something when you helped me that first night. Or they see us together and believe you to be my mate, or important to me. You're in danger because of me and I'm involved because of the jamboree business. So of course you're my responsibility."

"You need to go." She pushed him toward the door but he stopped, not wanting to be moved. Dario called, Gibson knew his ring and he picked up.

"I'll get back to you. I want you to look around, see what you can see. Any signs of surveillance and I want to know about it immediately." Gibson hung up.

She tried to push him toward the door again and he sighed. "You're not strong enough to move me and you're only going to make that slice on your back worse. Just stop."

She stepped back, the air between them, usually so hot, was now icy cold.

"What the fuck is wrong?"

"I'm apparently a weakling and a burden."

"What? I never said that." And that's when he realized they were totally in a relationship and she was his—for wont of a better term—girlfriend.

"I already told you I'm no one's responsibility and I'm not so weak I can't take on two full-grown shifter males and kick their ass. I hope they bled out on the sidewalk." She began to pace now, snatching her towel back and putting it around her body. "You're damn right they wouldn't be fucking with me if they hadn't seen me with you. But that's neither here nor there. It's done. They're trying to kill me, just like they're trying to kill you, and I notice *you* aren't living with your parents."

"Why is it that women always interpret words in the worst possible way?"

Her brows flew up as she spun, the towel nearly losing purchase, and then he remembered how much he liked what she had going on underneath it.

"You know, it occurs to me you either have a death wish or you've never been in a real relationship with a woman."

He felt a little of both.

"I'm not saying you're a burden."

"You're avoiding the issue."

Christ. "This is why I've never had a long-term relationship with a woman before."

"You don't even need a shovel to dig yourself in, do you? Astonishing. Go, Gibson. I don't want to fight with you right now. I ran four miles before I got attacked. So I was already grumpy. Then two shifters tried to kill me in the middle of a running path. Then I had to run home and not get caught. And now you're in here talking shit and being a dumb dude and I don't have the energy for it."

"You're being—" But he shut up when he saw the look on her face. Now he didn't feel so funny for all the times he poked at Max and Galen over the trouble they got into with their women.

"I'm not going anywhere. If you won't stay elsewhere, I'll stay here."

She sighed and walked past him, into the bathroom, slamming the door. Moments later the shower went on and he made a call to Dario.

"Across the street. The three-story brick? Yeah, on the roof."

"How many?"

"Two, maybe three. If there are three, two of them are related. She's not safe here."

"I tried to tell her that. She nearly ate my face off."

Dario laughed but quickly got himself under control. "What do you want to happen?"

"I want to know who owns that building. See if it's connected or if these cats are just sneaking up there. I'll let you know if I want extra people on this place in a bit. But I want another guard on her parents' shop and their home. I figure you can deal with them through her brother. Get me info on what happened to those cats on the trail. Dead? In the hospital and, if so, which one?"

"On it already. I'll get back to you as soon as I know anything. You want me to keep watch out here for the time being?"

"I want you on Max and Kendra. I'm fine here for now."

Dario hung up and Gibson took a deep breath before calling Max. But it was Kendra who answered so he filled her in.

"She can stay with us. We have the room."

"I don't want her with you. I want her with me, so I can keep a close eye on her."

Kendra laughed. "Oh, Gibson, you've gone and fallen for a complicated female. If I didn't like her so much I'd be laughing a lot harder. What did you do to piss her off?"

"You assume I made her angry."

"If you hadn't, when I offered our place you would have told me she was staying with you. You didn't. You said you *wanted* her with you. Which is different."

"I thought Max was the lawyer."

"Ha. He is. But I'm observant. And a woman."

"She thinks I said she was a burden and weak. When I really said she was my responsibility as one of my cats. And she was trying to shove me out of her apartment and I wasn't budging and I told her she wasn't strong enough to move me."

"This is after she took down two full-grown male jaguars on her own. Overcoming wounds of the like I hope to never experience firsthand. Hearing it from a man she's in love with and who she admires."

"Whoa, no one is talking about love. And I wasn't insulting her! I'm trying to protect her. She took what I said and twisted it into something ugly."

"It's a good thing you're so pretty because you are dumb. Almost as dumb as Max. Maybe more. Prove me wrong and grovel."

"Grovel? Me? For what? I didn't do anything but try to protect her! How is that a bad thing?"

"You already know. That's why you're so pissy and defensive. Go on. I'll fill Max in on what happened. Keep us updated. Grovel, Gibson. Believe me when I tell you that make-up sex is spectacular." She hung up, leaving him glaring at the phone in his hand.

The shower was still going in the bathroom so he took the liberty of rearranging her place to keep her a maximum distance from the windows. Grovel. Not in this lifetime.

Chapter Nine

The nerve.

She soaped up, wincing a little as the newly healed slash in her back tugged when she reached up to get her hair soaped up.

He normally did that. He had good hands, and while he was washing her hair, he gave a great scalp massage too.

But of course he was outside being a dick and not in here with her getting lucky. Boys could be so stubborn sometimes.

She wasn't weak. She didn't need protecting, though since this was a private conversation in her head, she could admit she sort of liked it when he got all protective. Being his focus like that was...it made her sort of shivery. Gave her butterflies.

On the other hand, feeling like a responsibility or a burden sucked.

She managed to finish rinsing off and get out. Her clothes were in the bedroom so she had to go out.

But he was waiting, on the bed. Her clothes at his side.

If he thought he was going to get in any naked, horizontal fun with her after all this stuff he did, he was out of his furry mind.

"I'm sorry."

She froze, eyeing him carefully.

"For what?"

She could see him count to ten in his head. "For hurting your feelings."

She grabbed a nearby robe and put it on. "Apology accepted. Now go."

He rolled from the bed, looking stupid gorgeous as he did. Damn it.

"I didn't say, nor did I mean you were weak." He got closer and closer, and her anger began to melt away. She shored it up as best she could.

"And when I said you were my responsibility, I didn't say it all. I mean, I only mentioned part of it. As Bringer, you're my responsibility because you're one of my cats. It's my job to protect you. To protect everyone. I take that very seriously." He licked his lips, and she didn't step back once he reached her and tugged on the belt of her robe.

"Stop that." She slapped his hand but he was undeterred. Probably because she hadn't slapped him hard enough. Easily remedied.

"What I didn't say was that I like you not dead. I like you safe. Because I like *you*, Mia Porter. I like you in my bed. I like you eating all the Oreos in the package in one go. It's already hard enough knowing I wasn't there for you yet again, but now you're more to me than one of my cats."

Well it wasn't a declaration of love and she wasn't expecting that anyway. But it was a genuine apology. And for a male like him to be so sincere and open meant a lot.

"How am I doing?"

She snorted. "Keep going."

He sighed. "Please stay with me. Or with someone else if you don't want to be with me. This place is exposed on three sides. Dario found a nest across the street on the roof. They've been watching you. Which means they know where you are. My place is fortified and well guarded."

"Fine."

"I'm forgiven?"

"You have a lot to learn about females." She walked past him to get dressed.

"I do."

"My suitcase is in the closet at the end of the hall. I need to call my family."

Mia knew there'd be some sort of come to Jesus with her family when she arrived at the shop the next morning.

Her mother called to her father and they both came down. "We need to speak with you."

She didn't even have her bag put down yet! Thank God she'd had coffee at Gibson's before she left.

"All right."

"Do you really think it's wise to continue associating with Gibson? With all this escalation of threats against your life, shouldn't you be getting the hell away from the de La Vegas instead of living with them?" Her mother shook her head. "It's bad enough you enlisted and went to Iraq. Bad enough you went to Los Angeles and then nearly got yourself killed there. But you come back here and get shot pretty much immediately! And now this new attack. Mia, this is dangerous and it's about the de La Vegas. They've done enough damage to this family, don't you think? It's one thing to go to dinner there and to attend a few jamboree events a year. It's another to…to consort with them while they put your life in danger."

Her father interrupted. "We know it's not your fault. We don't blame you. We just want you safe. You can go away for a while. Your uncle says you can come stay with them for a while up in Vermont. You'll be the hell away from here and safe. Let the de La Vegas handle this. They're better trained and it is their business after all."

She crossed her arms as Drew wandered into the room and froze. But to her immense relief he moved to stand next to her, not with their parents. A subtle but clear indicator of where his allegiances lay.

"What's going on? You okay?"

"Mom and Dad are telling me to stay away from the de La Vegas and go to Vermont for a while."

"Why is that a bad idea? Answer me that, Mia." Their mother glared.

"It's a bad idea because I have a life here. I have a job. I have friends and family. I have Gibson."

Drew raised his brows, but smiled.

"Yes, I'm living with him. But it's temporary until this all gets tied up. It's not some part of his nefarious plot to get sex for free and then dump me. Yes, they screwed Grandma over and that sucks. But I know it wasn't a single one of the de La Vegas who run the jamboree now and it has *nothing* to do with Gibson."

"Watch your mouth, young lady. Being involved with the de La Vega family has brought nothing but woe to us. And it's the same now, whether you want to see it or not. You're fine when you get back and then bam, you do something nice to help and look. You got shot! Here in our shop. And then last night you got attacked while you were jogging. All because of them. No good can come of this."

"Mom, I'm involved." She shrugged. "I know you're worried. I'm sorry this has touched your lives and this shop. More than you can know. If I could take it back, I would. But I won't now. Because I happen to like Gibson. A lot. This isn't about him being a bad guy. He's not going to get me pregnant and dump me. I'm careful anyway. And in case you hadn't noticed, I'm a strong woman in a completely different era."

Drew put an arm around her shoulders. "I agree with Mia. They care about her. About all their cats. If anyone can protect her, it's Gibson."

Their mother countered. "Fine job he's done so far."

She sighed. "Your feelings on the matter have been registered. I hear you and I respect that you're scared. Now, I've got work to do and I know you do too. I'll be living there until this is solved. And what I have with him isn't... Well I don't know what it is entirely. But I know he respects me. And I like him. Like him/like him. I'm asking that you respect that, and I'll keep you as updated as I can. You worry and I'm sorry about that. Believe me, I don't want to get shot again either. But I think you both need the jamboree and they want you. Drew needs that too. He's going to imprint, you know, and then marry. The Lennons are super involved in jamboree business. You'll have grandbabies and they'll be involved. Don't let yourselves keep out in the cold because of something that happened a long time ago. I don't think it solves anything, and I don't even know that Grandma feels that way anymore."

Her father nodded. "If you get killed, I want you to understand we will burn shit down. Do you understand? If the de La Vega family gets my daughter killed, there will be no end until they are all dead with you."

She blinked hard against tears that her normally sweet and good-natured father just declared a blood war should she get hurt.

She took his hands. "If I die, there's nothing to do. I'll be dead. But I'm working as hard as I can to not let that happen, and I swear to you right now that Gibson is doing everything he can to make sure that doesn't happen too. I love you both. I love this family. But I think it's time to end this nonsense between Porters and de La Vegas. They're sorry. The person who did it is long gone. Let the past remain there."

He'd really had no idea what it would be like to have her with him so much.

But a week later, as he was at the range with Jack, he realized it was better than he'd imagined. Which was scarier than anything he had to face as part of the job.

She was there when he woke up. Which he already knew he liked because she'd been spending three or four nights a week with him anyway. He liked her clothes in his closet, her scent lingering in the air.

He liked her toothbrush, not just an emergency one, but her real one, in his bathroom. She wasn't a visitor in his house, but a resident.

And so her life had clicked in with his and vice versa. Which he also enjoyed. She was there when he got home and it made his cat happy. Made the man happy too.

Jack was one of his brothers-in-law, mated to his brother Galen and their wife Renee. Jack was the Enforcer of the National Werewolf Pack. Sort of their national government. His job was pretty similar to Gibson's, so they'd developed a friendship as well. Jack was blond and ebullient. He seemed to love being around people. Essentially he was Gibson's opposite. But Gibson didn't hold that against him. In fact, it gave him a perspective Gibson sought out often, as it added to his own in really excellent ways.

"How goes it?" Jack cleaned his weapon before putting it in the case. "I ask because you used about eight times the ammo you usually do."

Gibson sighed. "I've got rogue cats out to kill me and now Mia. You know they attacked her again last week. And I'm really no closer to finding out what the fuck is motivating them. Though we do know the cats we've identified don't seem to have much of a recorded history before they joined Smithville. Their paperwork is thin. Sure they've got birth certificates and even school records, but no one seems to have remembered them before, and they came to Smithfield and took over rather quickly. I don't like it."

"Don't blame you. But a lot of shifters have had to hide. If they came from other cities, they could have lived as humans and then had some sort of experience that finally led them to join a jamboree. And an alpha is an alpha. You know if they arrived and one of them was more powerful than the sitting Alpha eventually a challenge would happen. That's how we are."

"I know. I've taken that into account. But even at that, people don't remember them. I've sent my men out to the schools these cats have diplomas from and no one remembers. Part of it is that teachers retire, that sort of thing. But come on. It's fishy."

"It is. Galen and I were discussing this just a few days ago."

"His dossiers have been a big help. He's a sneaky fucker."

Jack's snort was amused. "Yes. He's good at getting people to tell him things. So, Renee told me Mia is living with you now."

"If you only knew what it took to make that happen." He growled without realizing it and ramped it back.

Jack laughed. "What do you mean?"

Gibson filled him in on the argument and Jack laughed even harder. So hard Gibson punched him. Jack still laughed, but he managed to speak through it. "Ouch. Asshole. Don't get mad at me because you can't handle your female."

"Yeah, like you do."

Jack shrugged, a grin on his face. "I do in all the ways it counts. But Renee is her own woman. You'd be bored with a female who let you walk all over her. You're spoiled. You've dated around, fucked a lot. But you've never had this before. She's not just a chick you like to bang. No, she's far more than that. Also, your female is absolutely capable of slapping you back when you overstep and schooling you on what it is to love a woman. They're a big pain in the ass, in case you haven't noticed it yet. Fortunately they're worth the trouble."

"She's not my female."

"Oh she's not? So if I introduced her to Akio, you wouldn't care? I think they'd be a good match."

Akio was Jack's second, much like Dario was Gibson's. And there was no way any of that was going to happen.

"Only if you don't care if I kill him."

"Akio would be good to her. She'd be elsewhere and protected. They probably wouldn't even suspect that she was with the wolves." Jack shrugged.

"Fuck off."

"All right, so now that we've established that she's your female, what are you going to do about this rogue situation? Cade wanted me to let you know you have access to all our resources if you need them."

"Well, actually, I do have something to talk with him about. Is he around today?"

"Yeah. I'm on my way over there now if you want to tag along. We can grab lunch after."

Mia was cleaning out the back room at the shop when her phone buzzed.

The number was unfamiliar, but she recognized the last name.

"Mia Porter."

"Mia, this is Cade Warden. I'm the Alpha of the National Pack and I'd like to speak with you about something."

She knew who he was. Everyone knew who he was. The big bad wolf alpha who put down a major coup and took over from the old Alpha who'd been poisoned. He was also one of those super gorgeous males that made her so flipping happy she was a Were. Still he was mated and had a badass alpha female at his side.

And she had enough to handle with Gibson. Which made her smile because handling him was pretty fun.

"All right. What can I do for you?"

"We need a pilot."

She sat on the edge of the desk.

"We've got business travel and special deliveries to be made. A few times a month. We used a service but have had some problems with it and stopped using them a while ago. I travel to Washington State a lot to see my family, as well as Chicago and other major cities where my packs reside. And Grace, my mate, also travels a lot up and down the eastern seaboard. Does this sound like something you could handle?"

"I'm flattered you'd ask." Her heart pounded. "Aren't there wolves who could do this?"

"Some. Most of them I don't know."

"You don't know me."

He laughed, and the power in his voice made her shiver just a little. "I don't. But I know the person who recommended you. And I know the person who did your background check, who is my family."

"Gibson and Jack."

"Gibson has saved my ass a time or two. Jack more than that. And your record is exemplary. Would you like to come to our offices to meet with us face to face?"

Yes, she would. She scribbled down the address and arranged to meet him in a few hours' time.

And then she rushed back to Gibson's to get cleaned up.

He wasn't there of course. The house was quiet, which was good. She showered the dust and cobwebs off and looked through her clothes. She'd only brought a suitcase over that first night. But when she'd gotten home from work that following evening, she'd found all her clothes had been moved over by his people. They'd even put them in the closet and half the dresser.

He was so bossy.

She smiled as she chose a nice pair of pants and a blouse. She didn't need a dress or pantyhose for this, she was sure. And while she knew Gibson was behind the call, she also understood the job was hers to win or lose. Cade Warden wouldn't entrust his family or his wolves to her just because she was Gibson's, um, friend. He'd want to take her measure in person. Measure her genuine responses and personality, and if he had even a slight doubt of her, he'd thank her for her time and she'd leave without a job.

As she wasn't much for taking orders from anyone she didn't trust either, she'd do her own measure-taking.

Hopefully at the end of the meeting, she'd have a new boss and he'd have a new pilot.

Whatever the outcome, it felt good to be doing something to move on with her life.

She had no car so she figured she'd grab a cab. She wasn't familiar enough with where Cade's address was to risk being super late if she took mass transit over.

Dario was in the office when she got downstairs. He smiled at her when she came in. "You look nice."

She liked Dario Lennon. He was a smart cookie and was so loyal to Gibson she knew he'd lay his life on the line for him any time it was necessary.

"Thanks. I have a job interview. I'll be out of here in a moment. I just need to look a number up."

"Sure."

She turned the computer on and began to click through to find the number she needed. She'd dropped her phone in the toilet about twenty minutes after she'd arrived back at Gibson's, and it was hopefully drying out so she could use it again. But it meant having to look things up the long way when she'd already been totally spoiled by having the world in the palm of her hand.

"Something wrong with your phone?" he asked as she moved to the landline on Gibson's desk.

"I dropped it. Um, and it got wet."

He laughed. "I've dropped my phone in the toilet before. I don't keep it in my back pocket anymore."

She grinned. "Yeah."

But when she started to order a cab, he shook his head. "No."

She cancelled the cab and said she'd call back. "What do you mean no? Do you need me to have it pick me up a block away or something? Is this like the bat cave?"

He laughed again. "No, no, that's not it. Let me drive you."

"You have a job to do, Dario. I don't need a driver."

"I know you don't need one. But Gibson...well he'd want you to be driven by one of us. You don't need to take a cab. This is part of my job as it happens. Though really, no sweat to leave these pages and pages of useless data that still hasn't told us why the hell these cats want to kill you and Gibson. Where do you need to go?"

"I normally take the T or bus where I need to go. But it's an interview. I don't want to chance being late."

He stood and grabbed his keys. "So tell me about it. The job I mean."

She told him and his smile got even bigger. "I know exactly where National is."

The drive over was pretty easy, but it was nice not to have to worry about schedules, directions or parking. And Dario was fun to talk to. He wasn't overly nosy, but chatty enough that she didn't have to think too much about the interview.

When they arrived she turned to him. "Thank you. I appreciate the ride and the chitchat. You kept me from overthinking. That helped."

His smile brightened. "I'm glad. I don't think you need to worry. The Wardens are good people. You'll like them and I know they'll like you." He got out with her. "I'm going in to wait.

I can use Jack's office. We'll walk past it, so don't worry, you'll know where to go after the interview."

"You don't have to wait. I don't want to mess up your day. It's a short walk to the station from here. Just a few blocks away."

"Yes, I do. I have to. And I want to. For you and because I have several friends here and they always get new toys. Never know when there's a new weapon I need to talk Gibson into."

She laughed. "All right. Tell me if there's anything cool. I love weapons too."

He led her to the elevators and told the scary-looking male behind a desk that she was there to see Cade. The elevators opened and she moved to them, turning back to wave at Dario.

"Good luck, Mia."

It wasn't Cade who met her once she got off the elevator, but Grace. A female not even as tall as Mia. Elegant and beautiful. She'd heard from Renee that Cade's wife was gorgeous, but there was something so vibrant about her as well.

Grace moved like her name, but with power. She was an alpha wolf. Not just an alpha but the Alpha female of the United States. Being with her in person, it was quite easy to believe she was worthy of her position.

She also smiled warmly and took Mia's hand. "Hello! It's a pleasure to meet you. I'm Grace Warden. Cade asked me to bring you back. He's finishing up a phone call with his brother back in Seattle. Crazy stuff going on out there just now."

Mia knew of some of it. Witches disappearing, apparently kidnapped by mages who'd been bent on stealing their magick. Just as she knew it was one of the de La Vega sons who'd been aiding them and giving them information as to the whereabouts of Renee and Kendra so they could be taken. The reverberations of that still echoed through the jamboree.

"Would you like some coffee? I just made a pot so it's fresh and hot." Grace brought her into an office that looked very much like a living room. Several small couches with low tables dotted the space. The view of the river was pretty spectacular as well.

"Yes please. These offices are amazing," she said as she sat where Grace had indicated.

"I'm a doctor, you see. And I have a walk-in clinic downstairs, but this afternoon I'm finished with appointments. So I come up here to do alpha-type stuff but I don't want a traditional office. I have that down there if I want it. But up here I can have the kids with me if I want. They've napped on these couches more than once. Oh and if you're having a craving for Goldfish crackers, I've got several metric tons of them in the closet."

Mia laughed. "That's a nice thing. My parents own a wine shop, and my brothers and I grew up there on weekends and school holidays. During the summer my dad made us do inventory and all that stuff."

Grace brought over two mugs of coffee and some smaller containers. "Yes, they're in training for the long hours of running a Pack. Family business just like yours." She tipped her chin. "Cream and sugar if you like." She sat, stirring hers, adding a dollop of milk.

Grace took her in with eyes that didn't miss a thing. But her posture remained at ease. Shifter to shifter, things were going well. It was easy to relax around the other woman.

"So you're a pilot."

"I am. And you're in the market for one?"

Grace nodded. "We are. They used to have a service. But it's not totally safe. That ended up with my sister-in-law nearly dead. We like to avoid that, so we've been having one of Cade's old buddies come out to handle it when we need it. But he lives in Alaska and that's a hassle and it slows us down if we want to go right then. And sometimes it's a right then sort of thing. Can you handle that? Having only an hour or so before you have to fly one of us somewhere?"

"Barring any emergencies, yes."

"And what is your definition of emergency?"

Mia sipped her coffee and was glad to have something to do with her hands. "Someone in my family being in the hospital."

"All right, I can agree with that. I like your priorities."

She nearly laughed but didn't. She did, however, really like Grace Warden.

"You were decorated. In the military I mean."

Mia nodded.

"So if, say, one of us is threatened or under attack you could handle it?"

"I'm a full-grown shifter. I can handle most things. And when I can't, I know how to use a variety of weapons. But if you need a bodyguard, I don't know that I'm your gal. I've been recovering from...an attack. I'm in physical therapy for it now. But I'm a pilot who can react to danger and help protect you. Not a bodyguard. I'm not at a hundred percent."

Grace cocked her head, quiet for a moment. "What happened?"

She swallowed and told Grace the story. And when she was finished, she'd had no idea why she did so easily. Only that it had seemed natural to share with Grace.

But the words had flown from her, and with each one, the weight had become a little less.

When Mia had finished, Grace put her mug down, her mouth in a hard line. "Sometimes, Mia, I wonder why some things happen. Why such horrible beings exist. I'm sure people will tell you things happen for a reason. But that was senseless. It makes me angry that anyone would harm you. Or anyone else for simply being what they are. I'm sorry."

"So I understand if you'd rather have someone else do the job."

Grace sat back and waved it away. "You're able to fly still?"

"Yes. Cade described the aircraft you'd need me to fly. I can easily handle them."

"Then I have no need for anyone else to do the job."

Cade came in moments later and holy cow he was gorgeous. Like heart-stoppingly beautiful. The connection between him and Grace was brilliant. Mia was pleased just to look at them. They were clearly made for one another.

"We need to get Mia on the payroll immediately. I need to fly to DC tomorrow." She turned back to Mia. "The old Alpha of National, Templeton Mancini, was poisoned with a degenerative compound several years ago. He survived, but has a great deal of medical issues still. He's got his own doctor, of course, but that doctor is easily scared by Templeton."

Cade laughed and shook Mia's hand. "Grace is scarier than Templeton. I think Templeton loves that. So Grace goes and coos over him and takes the girls, our daughters that is, and everyone is happy."

And she walked out of the building three hours later with a job that paid enough to keep her in Boston and the beginnings of a new friendship. All in all, a very good day.

Chapter Ten

When Gibson walked through the door that night, the smells of something amazing greeted him. He followed the scent and found her in his kitchen, barefoot, her hair in two braids, a snug T-shirt not hiding the lack of a bra.

He approached and pulled her into his arms. "Best Wednesday night ever."

She grinned and kissed him soundly. "Not even over yet."

He kissed her again because he could and because having her there at the end of a long day made him happier than he'd probably wanted to admit to himself even a week before.

"Do you like lasagna? If not, fake it. I made two huge pans of it."

"A better question is who doesn't like lasagna? Smells really good. To what do I owe the pleasure of this meal?"

"Room and board."

He laughed. "The fact that you let me touch your tits makes up for that."

"Ha. You know, Gibson, you're a big marshmallow underneath that snarly exterior. I won't tell anyone, but I want you to know I know."

"I'm sure you're mistaken. But what do you mean?"

"I have a job."

"Really? Good news. Doing what?"

"As if you didn't know. I'm going to be a pilot for National. My first flight is tomorrow."

Damn, Cade moved fast. Gibson had only mentioned it to him that afternoon.

"I got a call when I was cleaning out the back room at the shop. Rushed back here, got my business face on. Dario gave me a ride, by the way. He wouldn't let me take a cab. He's a nice man."

Of course Dario gave her a ride. As if anything else was going to happen. He gave her a ride to the shop that morning, and if Gibson could have her in his or Dario's custody all the time, he'd have been more comfortable.

"Anyway, it was obvious they learned of me from you. I appreciate that."

"They wouldn't have hired you if they hadn't felt you were right for the job. You got it on your own merits."

"Of course I did. But Cade wouldn't have known about me without you. So thank you."

He shrugged. Happy that she was so happy.

"It's a quick trip. I'll be back by the late afternoon. Just to DC with Grace."

"I'm going to send one of my men along. Don't argue, people are trying to kill you."

"Grace said her personal guard would be going. Dave, I think she said his name was. I'm going to be carrying too."

He held back his growl. "Be that as it may. You'll have a guard with you. That's how it has to be so don't fight me over it. If I can't be with you, I'm going to send along someone. And I can't tomorrow, I'm sorry."

"I'm not interested in anyone having to give up their life to be with me." Her mouth hardened and he realized they were headed back to that place they'd been in before.

"Didn't I just say I couldn't? I have meetings all day. If I was giving up my life, wouldn't I have cancelled them all and gone with you?"

She eyed him carefully and he wanted to laugh.

"You take me from happy to turned on to exasperated and then back to turned on in zero to three seconds."

"It's a gift." She kissed him again and turned back to the stove. "I really missed being able to cook big meals. I figure I'll need to find a place with a giant kitchen. Dario's dad runs a property management company so he's got me looking at a few places."

He frowned at her back as she dug through his fridge.

"I went grocery shopping today. Really, Gibson, you need more than olive oil and Parmesan cheese to eat. You're a growing boy." She laughed as she pulled things out and put them on his counter.

"You can give Dario or one of the others a list, and they'll get it for you. The jamboree has an account at a few places nearby."

"I'm perfectly capable of grocery shopping. And as I told Dario when he tried that *we have an account here* business, I don't work for de La Vega. I pay my own way. You didn't pay for my food when I lived elsewhere, you don't need to now."

He didn't want her living anywhere else. There was no need for her to look for apartments when she was here. And they didn't know how long this rogue-cat thing would last after all. She shouldn't move out until he was sure she'd be safe. That wasn't right now.

"You should hold off on finding a place."

Suspicious, she turned to face him. "That so? Why?"

"Because those cats are still out there. Because you're safe here. I like it when you're safe. And you don't work for us, but you do live with me, and it's my fridge and I say I pay for groceries. I have a job. If you had a job and I didn't, would you expect me to pay for groceries?"

"Nice try. But I do have a job. I work for my parents and as of tomorrow I'm working for National. I get paid a base salary and then bonuses for each job. I have money in savings. Those cats won't always be out there. You're good at your job and you'll find them and everything will be safe and I'll still need a place to live. Joe is back in two days so I can't go back there. Or I could, but I don't want to sleep on his couch any longer than I have to. And he'll want to have ladies back to his place for sexytimes anyway."

He exhaled, trying to read her as she regarded him with a poker face. There was something going on in that head of hers and damned if he could figure it out. "I like you here."

She grinned. "Wasn't so hard, was it?" She turned and stirred whatever she had in a pot on the stove.

"Was there a doubt?" He kissed the back of her neck, his cat settling down as her scent hit his system.

"It never hurts to say it out loud."

This relationship thing was complicated.

"How long until the lasagna is done?"

She turned to look at the oven timer. "We've got another twenty-five minutes."

"What about what you're cooking right there?"

"I was getting ready to put it on a back burner and put a lid on it."

He slid his hands around her waist and up her belly to find her breasts unfettered by a bra. He sighed, smiling against her skin.

He pulled her away from the stove and over to the center island. Easily, he picked her up and sat her on the island, stepping between her thighs.

She kissed his ears, knowing how sensitive they were, loving the way he growled low in his throat. She'd been with him long enough to recognize his turned-on growl. She knew that because she'd heard the pissed-off growl enough to know the difference.

He pulled her shirt up and over her head. "I could feast on you all day long."

"Don't ruin your dinner."

His teeth grazed over her nipples, one and the other and back again until she pounded on his back, wanting more than that. Needing all he had to give.

He laid her back and pulled her jeans and underpants off. "I like the braids, by the way."

He had her naked on his kitchen counter and he commented on her braids. He made her laugh.

"What's so funny about that?"

"You still have clothes on and you are not inside me. Lame."

He shook his head but he pulled his shirt off and then undid his rig, divesting himself of his weapons and then his pants and more weapons.

"You're like a small army."

"Gotta be. Brigands about." He moved back to her but she bent to reach his cock before he could spread her thighs wider.

"I want this in me."

He pulled her from the counter and spun her body so she faced it. "Feet apart."

His fingers slid through the slick folds of her pussy, and he hissed as she pushed back against them when he dipped inside her.

"Greedy."

"Mmm."

But the head of his cock was nudging into her body as she got to her tiptoes to get him deeper. "More."

"Patience. I don't want to hurt you."

She angled herself and used her hands on the counter to push back, taking him in all the way in one hard movement. She shuddered as a small orgasm spread through her body, warming her.

"Christ. You're too much. Wait, wait."

"Don't want to wait, Gibson. I want you in me all the way. Hard and fast."

She knew he liked it that way. His animal side just beneath the skin as he thrust into her. Possessing her. His fingers digging into the muscle of her hips hard enough to leave a bruise for a few hours.

She liked it too.

He snarled as she tightened around him and unleashed his desire. Fucking into her so hard she had to lock her elbows to keep from moving forward.

In the reflection of the granite on the counters, she watched his face. The intensity of desire on his features, the light of his cat in his eyes. Hers rose in response, filling her senses with that twin nature.

And then he licked her left shoulder and she whimpered at how good it was. At how much he meant to her. She'd look for another apartment just to have a fallback, but she liked living with him. Liked waking up sore and warm because after he'd woken her to fuck at three a.m., he'd pulled her close and held her tight until the alarm went off the next day.

She liked him. Period.

But she wanted him to admit it out loud. More than his careful skirting around it. More than his nearly saying it. She wanted him to ask her to stay. Wanted him to ask her to live with him, not just because it made her safe or he could keep an eye on her. But because he wanted to be with her all the time.

He reached around and found her clit, sliding the pad of his finger over it in tiny circles. Over and over until she couldn't hold it back anymore, and she came so hard she brought blood when she bit her bottom lip.

His teeth grazed her shoulder and everything in her froze. Her cat seemed to roll inside her. She stretched her neck, exposing it to him in submission, and he growled, those grazing teeth suddenly grasping and biting the muscle.

She came again, nearly collapsing as orgasm crashed again and again as he joined her, her flesh still in his teeth. As he marked her.

He couldn't believe he'd marked her.

But once she'd bared her neck and offered herself, his cat pushed, the man didn't resist. He had to get his teeth into her skin, and when he had and she'd come again, he fell into her so deeply he knew he'd taken a step into a place he couldn't retreat from.

He rested his forehead on her shoulder, eyes open, looking at it. At the mark of his teeth in her skin.

He knew without asking that no one had marked her before.

Just as he knew he'd be thinking about that mark all the next day as she flew Grace to DC and back. And that he'd be waiting for her at the National building to give her a ride back home. Where he'd celebrate the first day of her new job.

Because she was far more than one of his cats.

It had been a good day. When she'd climbed into the cockpit of the Gulfstream, it had all come back to her in a rush. She'd fought back tears as she re-oriented herself. She'd flown the midsize private jets a few times over the years, and this was one of her favorites.

She could do this, she realized. She could fly planes and live the life she wanted to on her own terms, and those shitheads down in L.A. could fuck off.

Grace had settled in with her daughters and her bodyguard, Dave, along with Robby, one of Gibson's men assigned to guard Mia. Thank goodness the plane was a good-sized one so everyone would fit comfortably, giant shifter males and all.

Grace's daughters had come along with their mother to see Templeton, who in turn was delighted to be fawned over and jumped on and slobber kissed. He'd even played dolls with them, and in doing so, Mia had absolutely fallen for the charmer.

His mate, Carla, had also been wonderful. Chatting with Grace and Mia about a trip they'd recently taken. While Templeton wasn't strong enough to be Alpha anymore, he was still alive and had no plans to stop enjoying his life.

As they'd left he pulled Mia aside.

"It was a pleasure meeting you, Mia. I wanted to talk with you about something and I'm going to mess it up because I'm a man and I'm nosy and of course no one should have shared this with me, but shifters are a nosy bunch."

She'd known then he was talking about her attack and had looked to Grace, saddened that she'd shared a story Mia had told her.

"It wasn't Grace, I'll tell you that much." He looked over at Grace where she was packing her things up with Dave. "I don't know how much you know of the reasons why I retired and Cade took over. But I was dosed with a substance, a poison that led to the degeneration of several muscle groups. I was really bad off for quite some time, and while I'm recovered now, I get tired far more easily, and I'll never, ever have the strength I had before."

He paused and she tried to wrestle her emotions back.

"I was the Supreme Alpha of the United States. No one messed with me because I was absolutely the baddest wolf in the country. That's not bragging. That's the truth. And then I wasn't. I wasn't and not because I was an old wolf. Which is the natural order of things. It wasn't time to retire and hand over leadership to the next generation. It was because someone took my future away from me. With malice and intent to kill me. I will never be what I was before. It took me a long time to accept that. I was depressed for months. Poor Carla, I know I was horrible to live with. But she's no pushover and she kept shoving the truth at me until I finally accepted it. I can't be what I was before, but I can be something else. I can embrace what I have and live my life to the fullest."

He took her hands as she blinked back tears. "You flew today. How long has it been?"

She swallowed hard. "Five months. I haven't flown since before I left the air force."

"How'd it feel?"

She recalled that rush of joy when she'd taken off and they'd left the ground. "Marvelous."

He grinned. "Yeah. Don't let what you were before stop you from being the best what you are now. I'm around if you want to talk. I know what it feels like. I'm sorry as hell for what happened to you. I did call to rip a new one in the Pack down there. He should have offered to help. He's working with the police officer, who I also spoke to, nice boy. They're going to get some people on the men who nearly killed you."

She took the handkerchief he handed her way and dabbed her eyes with it. "Thank you."

"You're welcome. And I mean it. It was a pleasure to meet you. We'll see you next month. Keep the handkerchief." He patted her hand. "And say hello to Gibson for me."

Grace hadn't asked what he'd spoken to Mia about, though she was sure she guessed. But she didn't pry.

Instead, once they got back home, Grace gave Mia a hug and invited her to lunch the following week.

Mia had rediscovered a big part of herself that day.

So she came out of the elevator into the lobby to find Gibson standing there with a gigantic bouquet of roses, and the tears had come back, even as she grinned his way.

"Happy first day on the job."

She took the roses and tiptoed up to kiss him. Because it didn't matter if anyone saw. He brought her roses, damn it.

"You're getting really lucky later."

"My evil plan succeeded. Come on." He put an arm around her. "We have dinner reservations in forty-five minutes."

"Roses and food? You're a miracle to me, Gibson de La Vega."

He smiled, kissing her cheek before pivoting them toward the doors.

"Gibson, hold up!"

They both turned to see Jack coming toward them, holding a folder. "Some information here for you. Call me later." He stretched and kissed Mia's cheek. "Hey you. Thanks for handling the flight today."

Gibson's growl and tightening of his arm around her shoulder surprised them both.

Jack put his hands up and stepped back. "Just saying hello to Mia."

Gibson relaxed. "Sorry."

The mark on her back throbbed a little, and he turned to her, surprise on his face.

"Do you really think he was going to ravish me in the middle of the elevator lobby with your arm around me?"

He just looked back to Jack. "Thanks for the info. Appreciate it."

Jack winked at her and Gibson growled again.

Jack turned that brilliant surfer-boy smile on Gibson. "Fuck off, Gibson. You mess with Renee and Kendra all the time just to poke at your brothers and me. Get used to it. Your lovely Mia is far too pretty not to want to flirt with."

Mia laughed as Gibson hmpfed and led her out to his car.

"Hey, Dario." She waved as he got out and handed the keys to Gibson.

"Hey, Mia. Good flight today?" He opened her door and Gibson snorted, throwing his hands up and then pushing Dario from the way to help Mia up into the SUV.

She looked around Gibson's body to Dario. "It really was. It was a good day all around."

"Good. See you later." He turned to speak to Gibson for a few moments until Gibson got in the car with her.

Shifters were a territorial bunch, she knew. It was instinctual so those moments with growls and glares tended to happen from time to time, even with close friends and family. Generally it was accepted as something that came up and no one got really fashed over it. But they didn't usually occur unless the Weres were involved in a serious relationship. Which, she supposed, they were.

"So how was your day?" She breathed in the scent of the roses, smiling. "These are so pretty."

"Let's stop at home first for a moment. I need to make a call and the number is there."

"Everything all right?"

"Today we found out some stuff about the cats who attacked me. Us, I suppose. I need to call the Smithville Alpha, the new one."

She waited for him to navigate through a busy intersection, not wanting to mess with his concentration.

"I need to go down there. I'm only calling him as a courtesy."

"When? When do you plan to go?"

"As soon as possible. Tomorrow most likely."

"I'll take you."

He looked askance and then back to the road as they headed up the street toward his place.

"What? Max told me he had jobs for me from time to time as well. He said you guys have a jet. And even if you didn't, I could borrow the one I flew today. We could be there in a few hours. Back that same night if necessary. Or you could fly commercial. Show up hours early, get frisked, not be able to carry on board and then do it all over again, only on their schedule instead of yours. Everyone loves that."

He sighed and pulled up to the house.

"It could be dangerous." He got out of the car but she waited, knowing he was extra tense. She even let him help her down and got a quick kiss for her troubles.

"And I've been so safe and trouble-free of late. If only I had military training."

He groaned, put-upon, and they went into the house. "I don't want you in danger."

"Too fucking bad, Gibson. I already am. I have a skill you need. I'm offering it. I don't have to be back for four days so I have the time."

He held up a hand and dialed the number he'd had on his desk.

"Bob, it's Gibson de La Vega."

"Yes? What can I do for you, Gibson?"

"I'm calling to request permission for me and—" he flicked his gaze up to Mia briefly, "—four of my cats to enter your territory. I have to question some people who may have some answers I need."

"Permission is granted. But would you like my new Bringer to question them on your behalf?"

"No. Though your offer is appreciated."

"All right. Would you like transportation from the airport?"

"I've got that handled, but I would like to take a meal with you tomorrow evening if possible."

He eased the discomfort with that and Mia admired his political skill. He was playing whatever he was doing very close to the vest so the dinner offer would help Bob understand Gibson wasn't there with angry intentions toward Bob.

"Of course, yes. I'll have a dinner planned with me and my wife."

Gibson hung up, and she left the room to put the roses in a vase and let him call to set up the plane, because she knew he'd give in. It was the best option and he knew it.

Chapter Eleven

He took her to Amor, a restaurant she knew from various stories she'd heard about the de La Vegas. It was apparently their favorite restaurant, and Kendra had told Mia it was the place she really first started to fall for Max.

So it was special that he brought her there. Special that he'd kept his hand on the small of her back as they'd led him to the table.

"Do you mind if I order for you?"

Surprised he'd asked, she nodded. "Yes, that's fine."

He spoke to the server as she watched him in the candlelight.

"You'll like it. So how was it? Flying again?"

"I hadn't expected it to be as wonderful as it turned out to be. I was a little worried that it would be overwhelming or whatever, but it was like I'd never been attacked at all. It was...well it was good. Templeton sends along his hello."

"What'd you think of Templeton?"

She smiled. "I like him. He's a funny, flirty guy with a great wife and a pretty awesome outlook on life." She paused as they brought salads and glasses to go with the wine he'd ordered.

"Never been nervous to order wine before I met you. I hope you like it."

He was being remarkably sweet. "I don't think I've seen you nervous before. It looks a lot like confident on you." She winked and took a sip. "This is a very good red."

"I'm relieved."

The server poured them each a glass and left the bottle.

"He took me aside. As we were leaving. And he shared some of what had happened to him. He was very kind and gave me some very heartfelt and good advice." She sipped her wine.

"Do you want to talk about it?"

She liked that he didn't push. And he was a pushy guy. But there were times like just then where he got how hard it was for her to talk about it and he let her share as she could. Which made it easier to share the next time.

"He knows what it means to never again be what you were before. To have to live knowing you'll never be as strong. To know your life, your future, was stolen by people who don't deserve to be breathing."

He took her hand.

"Anyway, he just shared that and it felt good to be understood. Sometimes...well sometimes I know people care and they feel bad, but they can't know. You're a powerful male at his prime. You're strong and fast and respected. You are a badass no one is going to mess with and you've earned it. You can listen to me when I'm sad, but you can't *know* what it feels like to have your future stolen." She lifted her gaze to him and held it. "And I don't want you to. I wouldn't wish that on anyone. But it's lonely sometimes. He made me feel less lonely."

"I'm glad you met him then. And I'm sorry you're lonely. I wish I could make it better."

She snorted. For such a tough dude, he could be so very sweet. "You *do* make it better. Even when you're bossy and you say dumb guy stuff." She smiled because it was totally true. And he sat back, keeping her hand for long moments before they both started eating.

"Sixteen years ago my father ran the jamboree with his brothers. Like his father had done. My Uncle Tomas was the Bringer."

She remembered some of this vaguely. She knew he'd challenged the old Bringer. But that was what happened. It was part of their culture to have challenges to positions of power. Only the very strongest could lead.

"My other uncle did the books. He was the other second, like Galen is with Max. He uncovered that Tomas was embezzling jamboree funds. Seventy-four thousand dollars."

Gibson hated to tell this story, but how could he not? How could he hold back when she'd just given him that bit of herself? He'd have been a coward. And he was no coward.

"So my father confronted him and he denied it. Worse, he started to undermine my father and, through that, the entire jamboree. He accused my father of trying to push Tomas and his family out. They were about a third of the jamboree so that was a big deal. Tomas was very charming. He had a lot of friends, and a rift was formed because at first my father didn't want to air the story about the embezzlement. Tomas was his younger brother. He didn't want to hurt him. And he didn't want to drag the rest of the jamboree into what he felt was a family matter.

"But after a while he had to because it was tearing the jamboree apart. Then Tomas started talking about challenging my father and that could not happen. My father would have beaten him, but it would have broken him. So I did it. A call had been made and there was a gathering of the entire governing council. I stood up and challenged him for the position. And instead of choosing first blood, he chose a challenge to the death."

Gibson remembered the look on his father's face when Gibson called a challenge. Proud, most certainly. But he was torn. Sad. And pissed off because Gibson hadn't discussed it with him first.

Gibson hadn't because he'd known his father would have tried to protect him and ordered him not to do it.

But when Tomas had been so boastful and said he didn't want to bother with anything but to the death, Cesar's jaw had hardened, his gaze narrowing. Gibson knew now, as an older man, that his father had to let go of his brother at that very moment. In front of the whole jamboree.

She watched him with those big brown eyes. Never judging.

The server brought their steaks along with several sides and they ate for a while in silence before he continued.

"I can't understand. Why didn't he choose first-blood?"

A first-blood would have been a challenge that ended when the first person hit the floor and stayed there a certain amount of time. It could have ended that way.

"Pride, I believe. He was at his prime. My age now." Gibson snorted. "He was cocky and strong and powerful, and he wanted me dead. He'd stolen from our family and our cats, and he wanted to destroy my father and kill me. And I wasn't going to allow it, even though I didn't want to kill him. He was my uncle. Despite what he'd done, I loved him. He taught me a lot of what I know. I was one of his top men.

"And I won. I didn't just win but I won handily." It had been the shortest challenge in jamboree history. He'd had his uncle's blood on his hands and he'd hated it. But he'd done it. He hadn't wanted his uncle to suffer, even though he'd been such an ass. He hadn't wanted his father to suffer because Tomas

157

was his brother, no matter what he'd done. Like Carlos was...had been *his* brother.

And because of how quick it went and because he'd done it fast and clean, no playing, no teasing, it had solidified his support in the jamboree immediately.

"You were meant to be Bringer, Gibson. If you hadn't been, you wouldn't have won so fast and so completely."

His uncle hadn't even landed a single blow, though he'd tried. He'd underestimated Gibson all while overestimating himself. And it had been his undoing.

But the other cats had taken it as fate that he was meant to be Bringer. Tomas's wife had left that night with their children. Some of his other cousins had gone with them as well. It had taken two years for things to feel right again and he still missed his uncle from time to time.

"It was, as they say, what it was. I've done my level best to hold the spot with honor and strength. To do right by my cats and my family. We haven't always been able to do what was right or best. We hurt your family. My brother Carlos and one of my cousins betrayed us all and nearly got Renee and Kendra killed." He hated that so much. Hated that Carlos had done so much damage. Hated that he'd had to play a part in his final sentence, with his father at his side.

And part of Gibson hated that despite all the shitty things his brother had done, he still loved Carlos.

"You can't take responsibility for what other people do, Gibson. Only what you do."

"For all I know, Carlos could have helped those fuckers nearly kill you. My brother might have been the person who stole your future."

"It doesn't matter. His worst crime was what you had to do because of him. I hate him for that. His betrayal didn't just end at what he did to Kendra."

Of all the things he'd expected from her, that was not it. She continued to surprise him with how perceptive she was. How giving she could be, especially with him. He'd never really spoken of that night he'd interrogated Carlos with their father at his side. Of the final sentence. He and his father had shared that grief, but they hadn't spoken of it since then.

But he couldn't get drawn into that memory just then. He had other things to say. "I told you that because I think Bertram Simmons is really Tomas's son, Alberto."

Her eyes widened. "Get out!"

"I don't know for sure. But I was going over the footage for the millionth time. Of when they entered the lobby of the jamboree building. And when he turned a certain way...I'd played that part of the video over and over and over again. Something was bugging me but I couldn't figure out what. Then my father had come by to see Max and have him sign some papers, and he said something like, *that boy looks a little like Serafina.* That was my aunt. And I realized he did. Not very much like Tomas, but he had my aunt's eyes. He's the right age. The timelines are pretty close. Remember I said it looked like they didn't really have a past until about fifteen years ago? I could totally be wrong, but I want to go down there and see for myself. I want to go into their houses to scent. I want to speak to the remaining members of the Bringer's team and those around Bertram. I need to know."

She exhaled. "So you think this could be about them wanting revenge for you killing their dad? Fifteen years is a long time to wait."

"You should know more than most, jaguars are happy to wait and stew. We hold on to grudges a very long time." He shrugged slightly. "He was younger then, my cousin. But he took the jamboree over relatively quick after arriving there. It's in our blood, the power to lead. He could have just been biding his time. Or maybe he was going to live the rest of his life and something triggered this need for revenge and spurred him into action. I don't know. But I need answers. And this is why I think it's very dangerous and worry about you going."

"Too bad. I've got your back, Gibson."

"Dario has my back. That's his job."

"You mean something very different to me than you do to Dario."

Stubborn.

And he was glad for it. Because he wanted her there. Selfish or not, he wanted her there at his side when he went through all this. If it was his family, he'd still have to kill them if he found them. He hated it, but it was no less true or necessary. And she made him better, even when he knew what had to be done.

"Look, this is difficult because it's not just about the job. It's not some random cat pulling shit; this could be your blood. And I promise not to tell anyone and all, but you're gooey for the people you love. I know you'll do what's right. But I know there's a cost and I don't want you to pay it alone."

And what could he say to that? She touched him in ways he'd never really imagined before he'd met her. This hard-assed little cat with her perceptive gaze and wicked aim had stormed into his life and made herself at home. There was no fighting it anymore.

"If you come with me you have to obey me. You'd be like any other member of my team."

"I know how to take orders, Gibson. Jamboree discipline and order is a lot like the military. I know what that is."

"So why don't you obey me at home?"

She laughed, delight washing over her features and evoking an answering smile.

"Home is different. You're not my Bringer at home. You're my man at home. I don't have to obey you there if you're being a dumbass."

He shook his head. "Things would be more fun if you did obey me."

She shivered at the way he'd lowered his voice. "Don't go using your sex voice to get me off track. I do obey you in that way. It's really in my best interests as you're quite awesome at anything to do with naked."

He sighed. "What am I going to do with you?"

"I hope you've got some ideas. If not, I'm sure I can think up a few things."

"Let's stop at Max and Kendra's a moment. I want to talk with him about what I found out today. I can drop you at home first if you prefer."

She liked that he referred to his place as home for the both of them.

"No, that's fine. Kendra's cool. Plus, I want to hear what you've got planned. Just in case you try to ditch me or something."

He snorted. "I'm not a weak-ass kitten. If I didn't want you going, I'd say so and risk your wrath. As wraths go, it's pretty spectacular anyway."

"I must tell you that your compliments are totally unique. Awesome. But only you could say those things and make me know you mean them as a positive."

"Hm."

He drove and she curled into the seat, just watching him. She was full to the point of bursting. Warm. Satisfied and in love.

Oh she'd tried to tell herself it was a relationship and eventually her like would be love. But it already was and more than that, she was imprinting on him. There was no going back from how she felt about Gibson. Not anymore. And she didn't want to. It didn't matter what her family thought. She loved them and wanted them to approve, but she wasn't going to give him up.

"Wow, this is their house?" She sat up a little to take it in better. She sighted the guards. "Do you think three guards is enough?"

"You can see them?" He put the car in park and turned to her.

"Sure." She pointed. "There on the left, over there in that tree and then north, at the back of the yard. We should have brought them something to eat."

He snorted. "God. Don't say stuff like that. They have breaks to eat. Their job is to guard the alpha pair, not to have a quilting bee."

"You're a dick. I'm sure they'd appreciate a sandwich."

"First of all, I can guarantee Kendra has been out there messing with their schedule with her cookies and snacks as it is. I can't boss her around. But you, missy, you I can. You said you'd obey me."

She laughed then. Who'd have thought that he'd have such a great sense of humor?

"Har."

"Second—and this is more interesting to me than Kendra giving my men brownies behind my back—you can see them. Why is that?"

"What do you mean? They're right there."

"Contrary to whatever you might think, *bebe*, they're well hidden. It's their job to be."

"Well I can see Matt right there." She pointed.

"Yes, you're supposed to. He's the clue that they're being guarded. But the others? Not so much." He looked out again and then back to her. "Tell me how you saw them. What drew your attention to them?"

She cleared her throat and thought about it. "The one in the tree I saw when he moved a little. I can't see him now, though. I caught the movement more than him. And then I focused and saw him clearer. The one to the left of the house, it was his eyes. I caught the gleam. Must have been a reflection of the headlights."

"Christ, Mia, that was like a millisecond. People don't see that stuff."

"I'm not people. I'm a jaguar."

He took her hand. "No, really. You're very perceptive."

"Would you have seen them?"

"Yes. But I'm the Bringer. I've been trained for it. And this is more than military training so don't tell me that. You have a gift." He kissed her knuckles, leaving her flustered and flattered.

"Well, um, thank you. And might I add that it only gives you yet another reason to take me along to Tennessee."

"And the last one. How did you see him?"

"Her." She peered through the windshield again, waiting. "Ah, there. She needs to use something on the scope of her rifle. It's shiny in one small spot. Likely where the matte has worn away. I can help her with that."

He shook his head, leaning across the center console to kiss her soundly. "You're amazing."

"Thank you." He left her breathless and warm as he went around to get her door.

Kendra smiled and drew Mia into a hug when they came in. "Hello! What a nice treat to see you both."

Gibson kissed her cheek, and it was Mia who found herself digging her nails into her palms. This was his sister-in-law. She had to repeat it a few times, but Gibson turned to see the expression on her face and he had the audacity to grin.

"Where's my brother?"

"Galen is here. There's some sort of sport thing happening on that 70-inch television he convinced me it was so important to buy. It's not even a current thing. It's some old Super Bowl game for God's sake." She shook her head, but she was smiling.

"Good, I need to talk with Galen too."

"Is this work stuff?" She frowned.

"Yes."

"Well come on then. Renee!" She looked back to Mia. "I know it's hard to see him hug me. Now that I'm a cat sometimes it happens to me too. I see Max hug or be affectionate with women and it makes me see red. Even our relatives and friends. It's odd. Gibson knows it and he pokes at Max. I find it pretty funny because Max tries to pretend it's nothing but he bares his teeth. Ha! Mister self-control loses his shit and it makes me laugh. I can't help it. I'm sort of mean that way." She patted Mia's hand.

"I grew up this way. It's...I never expected..." Mia shrugged, not knowing how to explain it.

"The de La Vega males are all unexpected I've found. They're all great big softies once you scratch the surface."

There was a crash and they all rushed down the hall to find Galen and Max brawling. Renee stomped in and pulled Galen off by the ear. "You two! Honestly. Stop breaking his nose. It's going to get crooked and he has such a pretty face."

Gibson grabbed Mia's hand and squeezed it a moment, the hint of a smile on his lips.

Mia leaned close and told him, "My brothers once got blood all over one of my mom's rugs, and she made them both camp out in the backyard in a tent for a week."

Kendra's gaze lit with amusement. "Your mom sounds pretty awesome. Max, maybe your father needs to make you and Galen work out of the parking lot instead of letting you in the building. He's still mad you two broke the chair in his office."

Jaguar males tended to be very physical with those they trusted and loved. So it often meant brothers and friends would get into knock-down, drag-out brawls over silly stuff. Because they healed so fast, it wasn't unusual to include broken bones.

She was glad Gibson didn't seem to do it like Max and Galen, though. She supposed he had less freedom to do such things because he was the Bringer. He was very serious about his job, and if he started popping people in the nose, it might seem like punishment instead of roughhousing.

Max and Galen picked up the stuff they'd knocked over and then looked to Mia and Gibson. "Hey you two. Come watch the game with us. Super Bowl 43."

"Nice! But first I have work-related things to discuss."

Max's smile dimmed as he got serious. "All right. Let's all sit down."

They did and Gibson briefed them on the info he'd discovered and the plan to go down to Tennessee the following day.

"I'm going to take Dario and leave Matt and Robby here on you two."

Max nodded. "Fine, fine. Take however many cats you need to. I can't believe I missed the Bertram/Alberto connection."

"I didn't see it either." Gibson shrugged.

"I want you to report back frequently. And if for a moment you think Bob and the new jamboree leadership has anything to do with it, you'll get the fuck out of there and contact me."

"This can't go unanswered." Gibson paused to take a drink.

"We don't know for sure that it's really Tito. It's a hunch."

"Your hunches are spectacularly accurate, Gibson." Max blew out a breath. "Mia, you stay safe, please."

"Of course."

"And keep Gibson safe too." Renee tipped her chin toward Gibson.

She grinned, but it was more feral than amused. "I will."

"I'm going to hold off telling Dad. It's best to wait. If we have to hurt him with this all over again, I'd rather be totally sure."

Max agreed. "Yes, that's best I think. You've gone up the chain correctly by telling me. Mia, don't get hurt. I'm totally afraid of your grandmother."

Mia laughed as the tension in the room eased a little. "She'd totally eat you up and spit you out if she had to."

"It's a good trait in a female." Max looked to his wife with a smile.

Two steps inside the front door and Gibson had his hands on her as he pressed her against the wall, holding her there with his body. The need was always between them, just waiting to explode. But that evening had been... Well he'd known they'd stepped into a whole new stage of their relationship.

She understood him in ways he'd never experienced outside his family. She didn't judge him for what he had to do. And when she did judge, it was legitimate, even if he didn't agree.

"You're a singular female," he managed to say as he broke the kiss.

"I am?" A smile quirked up one side of her mouth and he had to kiss it.

"Yes. Goddamn, I want you, Mia."

"Take me then."

He pulled the front of her blouse open, sending buttons flying. She gasped, and the sound caressed his skin, driving his cat mad with need. Her bra was open just seconds later and he dipped to taste her skin, growling when she tugged his dreads. As if he was going anywhere now that his mouth was on her nipple.

She moaned. "I'm going to knock this photo off the wall. My head is too close."

He picked her up, his mouth still on her, and she held on as he walked her into the living room and deposited her on the arm of the couch. "Now, I can't very well eat your pussy with your pants on."

She made quick work of them and stood there bare to the bone. What she felt was in her gaze, and it humbled both man and cat. She gave herself to him like the gift she was. And there was no denying what she was. Not then. Not when she'd been so raw and honest with him.

He dropped to his knees before her, hugging around her waist, simply breathing her in for a moment. Her arousal spiced the air, teasing his senses. "Sit on the couch arm. I'm going to lick you until you scream and then I'm going to fuck you. I've wanted to bend you over this couch pretty much since I met you."

She sat, her fingertips tracing over his brows, down his nose and over his lips. "You're beautiful."

He snorted, but he knew she meant it. And that humbled.

He kissed her ankle, always so delighted by the softness that wrapped the iron-hard strength of muscles just beneath. Up her calf to that spot behind her knee that always made her gasp. And she did.

Up the velvet softness of her inner thigh and to her pussy where she was desire swollen and slick. Just waiting for him. He growled against her flesh and she gasped. This was his. She was his and that was that.

He took a long lick. Over and over as her taste owned him. Marked him as assuredly as his teeth had marked her shoulder. He scooted her a little forward so he could get at her better, holding her open with his shoulders as he went back to her cunt. Beautiful as the rest of her. Her taste dug in with sharp claws as he tickled the underside of her clit with the tip of his tongue. His thumb slid back and forth over her asshole, and she shivered as he kept licking and sucking.

Her hand was on his shoulder for purchase, and he knew he'd have half-moon marks from where her nails were digging into his flesh. His cat approved of her for that. His female marking him, letting anyone who looked close know there was a female who'd claw and scratch if anyone got too close.

She shook all over as he sucked her clit into his mouth, in between his lips over and over and over until she exploded all around him, as he eagerly lapped her up while she calmed a little.

He stood moments later, and she watched through half-open eyes as he undid his belt and jeans to pull his cock out.

There was no time to get undressed. He needed her right then. He helped her up and spun her to bend her over the back of the couch. The arm was too low to get in deep and hard.

And that's what he needed.

He was inside and hissing at how good it felt within the space of two breaths. She pushed back against him, taking him in all the way. He looked at the line of her back. Her scars were fading more each day as she got better, as her outside healed. He knew the inside would take longer.

She was elegant, this little cat. Petite but strong. Demanding. Vicious when she needed to be.

Her skin glistened with sweat as he fucked into her body. Her muscles bunched and relaxed under the hands he had at her waist to control his speed and depth.

His cat was restless just beneath the skin. Wanting to claim. He needed to run with her, he realized. But right then? He leaned down and licked. Licked at the salt of her skin, groaning as it mixed with the spice of her pussy, still on his lips.

His mouth watered and then he bit hard. Marking her. On purpose this time. With full knowledge and desire to do so. This was not merely a heat-of-the-moment bite. He was marking her as a declaration of intent.

She gasped and said his name so very softly, and yet filled with so much emotion that he couldn't hold back a second longer. He increased his pace, harder and harder, faster and faster until he spun finally over that edge and came so hard he had to close his eyes against it.

Chapter Twelve

"She's carrying? You two are a perfect match," Dario muttered as they waited for her to get into the rental car.

He'd loved to watch her fly the plane, and she'd been kind enough to let him sit in the cockpit with her for some time as she did. Her attention was totally different when she worked. Intense at times. So intense it was like nothing else existed but that.

And they'd arrived. She'd suggested they do so an hour before he'd told Bob they were arriving. She was sneaky that way. Another trait he liked about her. She'd handled the rental car, insisting on keeping that low profile.

"She's certainly not a female who needs to be babied or taken care of." She was self-sufficient. His mother had said she had moxie and that was totally true. Independent enough to drive him crazy. But there was something amazing in the way she let him take care of her when it mattered most.

She had baggage. As did he. But she was a full-grown female who knew her mind and that was the sexiest thing ever.

She got in. "All right. The paperwork is fine. Let's go."

It was Dario who drove them to the first stop, Bertram's home.

"Park a few blocks away. Let's take the alley. I don't want to be seen just yet."

She approached with him, pausing to peek into the trashcans. Which were full. "Karl, I want you on this. Bring this into the garage or the backyard and look through the bags."

"I can't believe they haven't done this by now," Mia said quietly.

"They're having to start from scratch. This is a small jamboree. I think it's more a matter of just not having the training to run an investigation rather than incompetence or collusion with Bertram."

She snorted but held her tongue.

They looked around the backyard and then let themselves into the house. The nearest neighbor was on the other side of a very large hedge and fence, and the houses were on big lots so he was hopeful they hadn't been noticed.

"I'll take these rooms. Dario, you take the second floor. Mia, the basement."

She nodded and he wanted very much to tell her to be careful. But he didn't because he didn't say it to Dario and he knew she would be anyway.

He wasn't more than five minutes into searching the kitchen when she came back up the stairs. "Found a hidey-hole."

He called Dario and they headed downstairs. There was a washer and dryer at one end and a pool table at the other. And a panel she must have removed just behind the washer.

"There was a lockbox in it." She indicated the large box on the pool table. He popped the lock and opened it up to find pictures, birth certificates, property deeds and other types of paperwork.

Most of it was for Bertram and Sharon Cole. But the pictures were another story.

"It's him." Gibson held a picture of his uncle with his grandfather and had to swallow back the lump in his throat.

Dario took the property deeds. "This is for the house we're in now. But there are others. They might offer some clues as to his current whereabouts."

"Call it in to Galen so he can look into it."

Dario moved to do exactly that.

"No passports," Mia spoke up. "And the birth certificates are photocopies. It's easier to carry off a fake with a photocopy. That's probably how they got the original documents with the new names."

"Why assume they had passports?"

"They had a hidey-hole. They have all these other documents. I bet they had a lot of cash stashed around too. It costs a lot of money to run."

"He didn't run though. He's orchestrating this entire thing."

"While he's on the run. Not to South America, I never thought that story was true. But he's away from home. He can't use his bank accounts. They ran before too. He's got to have been prepared enough to have passports just in case. I would have. You would have too."

Gibson nodded. He did indeed have stashes of cash here and there should he ever have to run.

"Let's see how many other hidey-holes we can find."

In the end there had been three more hidden stashes around the property. Mia had a great eye. And apparently a penchant for great hiding places.

As they'd had all the assorted things spread out on the bed of their hotel room, he'd turned to her. "How did you find them all?"

"I was a teenage girl. I had a hidey-hole of my own. I'm sure my parents didn't care about my diary, but I have two brothers and they would have. So I learned to hide things. And I got some training for it."

"As a teenage girl?"

She laughed. "No, silly. How to spot someone who might be strapped with a suicide bomb. Or how to notice when cars looked a little different, or the road. Lots of IEDs killed our soldiers, you know. Anyway, it wasn't what I did personally, thank God. But I thought the training would be useful and so I took it. I learned a lot, but I never imagined I'd need it back here."

"Whatever the reason, I'm glad for it."

She looked at him, reaching out to touch his face. He leaned into her palm, settling a little at the simple gesture. "I'm glad too. It's hard for you." She kissed him softly. Dario was off in his room working with the others on all the data they'd found that day, so it was just them and he could be soft.

She gave him that. That solace.

"I wish it wasn't this way. But you didn't make it so. They started it, but you have to end it. And I'm sorry. But I have confidence in you. The Bringer is the heart of the jamboree. Sometimes justice comes with blood."

He swallowed words he didn't know how to say. They'd declared war when they came into de La Vega territory. There was no way around it. And no way around how he had to respond.

With that spooky second sense she had, she seemed to understand he needed to back off and process the emotions that'd been stirred that day. "Take a shower. I'll keep looking through this. You're supposed to be meeting Bob in forty-five minutes."

She turned back to the bed, sifting through the papers and making notes.

"You should join me."

She rolled her eyes. "We'd be really late if that happened."

"Sure, but it'd be worth it," he tossed over a shoulder as he went into the bathroom.

He had incontrovertible evidence that Bertram Cole was really his cousin Alberto. He sighed as he soaped up. He hadn't wanted it to be so. He'd wanted it to be about something other than this. Anything other than this, damn it. He hated that his father would hurt anew over it. Max was on his way over to their parents' home right then to tell him face to face. He felt for Max, who also wanted to avoid hurting Cesar.

They'd met with a few neighbors and went to the school Tito's kids had attended. They'd disappeared the day before their father had sent all those cats into de La Vega territory.

What a fucking mess this whole thing was.

Yet, what a boon she'd been on the trip. He'd thought he'd ceased to be amazed at how good she was at things, but that day had shown him she was even better than he'd thought. Her military training had been a blessing. He wasn't sure he'd have found everything without her eye.

And he liked having her at his side. Liked knowing that she understood how upsetting it was for him. Liked that she pushed on, knowing it had to be done. It was entirely new for him, letting himself depend on another in such a way. Sure he was fine with the investigation and the work of a Bringer. But she knew him on a different level and that was comforting in a way he wasn't quite sure he understood fully.

"So, for fifteen years Alberto built a base of power here. He bided his time and gathered resources. This was not a momentary explosion of anger. This was premeditated. With their foray into de La Vega territory without permission they flirted with war, but when they shot me they declared it."

But not openly and honestly. And that offended Gibson. No, everything his cousin had done was cowardly. And cowards were far worse than other kinds of threats because cowards had no core values. They had no honor. One couldn't palaver with a coward because you couldn't trust their word or deed. And if you had no options to avoid war, you had to fight and you had to win.

And he could see Bob understood that clearly.

"Whatever you need from us, you have. We take responsibility for what Bertram, um, Alberto and our other cats have done. But we ask for your mercy."

He'd checked in with Max before they'd arrived, and his brother didn't want to punish Smithville for what their cousin and his men had done. *If* they found no one in the current leadership or general membership was involved. They were a very small jamboree. Less than ten remaining members after Alberto had left. Each member was being investigated by de La Vega and if a single shred of evidence was raised, the tenuous deal they made now would be null and de La Vega would extract their price.

"My Alpha has decreed that so long as no one left here is in league with, or, having aided our cousin, you will be spared. But if we find out different, Bob, you know the price."

The other Alpha nodded. "I do. Thank you."

They finished their dinner, having questioned Bob and his inner circle, and went back to the hotel.

"I don't think he's here in Tennessee," Gibson said in the dark as he and Mia lay naked, limbs entwined.

"I don't think so either."

"Tell me why."

He'd taken to doing that. He asked her opinion, but wanted to know how she came up with it. Gibson understood the world in ways most didn't. He liked to know the why of things, not just the facts. It made him even better at his job and it flattered her that he cared to know.

"Jamborees are like the military. When they're run well anyway. There's a clear chain of command. Rules of conduct. Certain people do certain things. These cats who attacked you are true believers, but I don't know that any we've seen so far have been strong enough to continue to run this operation without a leader. And not over the phone." Cats didn't work that way anyway. The power of an alpha was far stronger in person. "He's in Boston or nearby."

"This is personal for Alberto. He wants to see the carnage firsthand. It won't be enough to get a report."

She agreed.

"We need to declare a hunt."

She stilled as his fingertips continued to brush up and down her forearm. She'd only heard of such things as stories. "I never...I guess I thought those were old wives' tales."

"My brothers and I have done it twice."

He didn't elaborate, but she was sure they'd succeeded.

"What can I do?"

Lauren Dane

"This is not yours. The hunt will be me, Galen and Max. I have a feeling my father will join in as well."

"All right. What can I do other than the hunt?"

"You're doing it. But you have a job. You have to fly people around, and truth be told, I like that you'll be out of harm's way as much as possible."

Possible. Bah. If he needed her—and she'd decide that for herself—she'd be there, job or no. And she'd misjudged Grace Warden greatly if the other woman wouldn't see it as far more important to be at Gibson's side in a time of need instead of flying here or there. She'd heard stories about how Grace helped Cade in a challenge when he'd been dosed with a biological agent that would have killed him had she not come up with an antivirus that had saved his life.

"Hm."

He sighed. "You're going to do whatever you want. But you can't come on the hunt. It's not for...I don't want you to see it."

"Is it bad? Do you think I'd judge you?"

"No, it's not that. I don't think you would. I think you understand why this is necessary. But in a hunt the beast runs riot, even when it wears the man's skin." He recited the lines from an old story and it gave her a shiver.

"I need to not be worried about anything but the hunt. I need you away from it and safe so I can give over to it. Do you understand?"

She turned to face him. "Yes. I do. But I'm here when you come back."

He hugged her to him. "I know. Thank you."

Chapter Thirteen

Her brother Joe had returned and she was on the way over to her parents' to have a celebration dinner. She hadn't seen much of them since she'd started her new job and after their discussion with her about living with Gibson. But she loved them and missed them and it was time to talk with them more honestly about just where this thing with Gibson was going.

Joe stepped out onto the porch and caught sight of her, waving. She'd wanted to come alone, or with Gibson, but Gibson was at a meeting with his brothers to discuss some new information they'd found that afternoon. He'd offered to cancel to go to the dinner, but she knew the longer this situation went on without resolution, the worse he'd feel about it. He wanted things to be done and she agreed it would be better that way.

Not that she cared about the feelings of this cousin and his family. Alberto had put them all in danger with his actions. Not to mention he'd tried to kill Mia as well as Gibson. He had to be put down like the rabid animal he was.

But Gibson had insisted that she have a guard with her at all times so Robby rode out with her that evening. He'd politely declined going in for dinner. She knew it was a guard's job to keep in the background, but it still felt weird.

Robby laughed. "Really. It's easier. Your family would be more nervous with me inside and I'd be distracted. I appreciate the invitation, though. I have a cooler with food and drinks."

He came around to let her out of the car, scanning the area, and stood back. "You know where I am if you need me."

"Thank you."

She headed up the walk where Joe had come out of the house and stood on the porch.

"Who's that?" Joe tipped his chin at the car as he gave her a hug.

"My bodyguard. Let's get inside. He'll get nervous with me out in the open."

"What the hell, Mia? Mom and Dad told me a little, but clearly not the whole story."

They went inside, and she locked the door behind herself and kept him off to the side as she filled him in on everything.

"Holy shit. Mia, this is trouble. This cat is trouble."

"Of course he is. That's why they're trying to find him."

"So why not stay away until they do?"

"Because Gibson is my man. I'm in love with him, Joe. And I can help him so I do. He won't let me do much really, so get that look off your face. If you think you all are protective, you have no idea what he's like. Believe me, I'm as safe as I can be under the circumstances."

"You love him? Jesus."

"I do. I'm imprinting. He's...I didn't expect him. If you'd asked me three months ago who I'd end up with, it wouldn't have been him. Or anyone like him. But now I can't imagine it not being him. All I can ask is that everyone respects that. He's not Silvio."

"I was just saying that."

180

Her grandmother spoke as she came into the living room. She tipped her cheek and Mia stroked her own along it. "Hey, Grandma."

"Come into the dining room. I'm about to talk about some things you'll find interesting."

Joe widened his eyes as Lettie turned and left the room.

Mia shrugged. You never knew what their grandmother would say or do so she just braced herself.

Her mother waved, happy to see her when Mia came through. Her father kissed the top of her head when he came in from the garage with milk from the outside fridge.

"Just in time. The roast is ready."

"Nice." She grabbed a sliver of the meat when she moved to sit, and her dad whacked her fingers with a spoon.

"Manners."

She grinned, sheepish.

Plates were filled and small talk was made, no one mentioning her trip and her grandmother remaining silent about this revelation she had in store.

"Tell us." Her mother finally spoke after they'd had a few minutes to eat.

Mia gave them a quick overview of the trip. She didn't provide a lot of details because some of it was stuff she knew Gibson didn't want to be common knowledge, and while she knew her parents could be trusted, it was just better if they kept it unspoken.

Her mother slammed her fist on the table.

"He's not good for you. From the first moment you met him you've been in danger. I don't approve."

She sighed, wishing things were different. But they weren't. "I know you don't. And I'm sorry because I want you to like him. He's a good man. And I'm in love with him."

Her mother blew out a frustrated breath. "And how does he feel? You're younger than he is. He's got more experience. You can't go loving a male like that. He has other priorities."

"You don't even know him, Ellen." It was Lettie who spoke that time.

Mia sent a grateful look to her grandmother before continuing. "I believe he loves me too. And I believe he's imprinting. He...he's marked me."

Her father scrubbed his hands over his face and muttered something incoherent.

"This isn't what I want for you."

"Mom, I know. It's not ideal. But it's not his fault. This whole thing is from the outside. He has to protect the jamboree. When he does that, it's all of us he keeps safe. Can't you see that? If you only knew the price he paid for the cats in the jamboree. For his family. All I can ask from life is an honorable man. I have one."

"Honorable! This is why I have serious reservations about being involved with the jamboree again on a regular basis. All this constant drama and violence. Not to mention the harm they've caused your grandmother and our family. Have you given no thought at all to that?"

She knew her mother was angry, but it was a slap and it hurt.

Lettie put her fork down and wiped her mouth carefully. "I've had lunch with Imogene several times. I quite enjoy her and the truth of the matter is, there is no one left in that jamboree who had a thing to do with what happened to me. I believe quite strongly that none of them would do such a thing to anyone. Imogene is a good mother. Her sons are not the same as Silvio."

"Except for Carlos. The one who sold information to the human hate groups like the one that nearly killed our daughter. Does no one remember that?"

"Mom, please. Let her speak." Joe squeezed Mia's hand briefly.

Lettie was the one to rap knuckles on the table this time. "What's past is past. It happened to me and I have accepted Imogene's apology. I think you're totally wrong about Gibson and Mia. Mia is strong. She's a smart woman who knows what she wants. She's not some silly young thing who doesn't know the difference between lust and love. I trust her with this and I think you should too."

It was unexpected, to say the least. But really, that's who Lettie was. She spoke her mind, even when it wasn't what everyone else thought or said.

Drew cleared his throat. "As you know, I've been with Stacy for a year now and I've grown really close with her family. First, Mia's not the only one who's imprinting. We're going to do the joining in the fall. We're saving to buy a place together."

Mia raised her glass. "Congratulations!"

There was much talk as their mother rushed over to hug him and ask a thousand questions. It took the heat off her for a bit, which made the news even better. She liked Drew with Stacy. They were a good couple and she'd be good to him.

"More roast?" Joe put some on her plate, winking. "Hold on, punkin. We'll get through this. Grandma is on your side."

"What about you?"

He snorted and shoved a huge forkful of potatoes into his mouth. Once he'd finished inhaling it, he shook his head. "I'm always on your side."

"Okay, enough about the joining for the time being. I had another point." Drew cleared his throat. "Dario is Stacy's brother, as you all know. And he's Gibson's second. He respects Gibson. Trusts him with his life. And I trust that. I've seen Gibson look at her, Mom. He looks at her like she's something miraculous and precious. I should hope *that's* what you wanted for her. A man who adores her and would give his life for her."

She mouthed a thank-you and he nodded back.

Mia's grandmother cleared her throat and everyone quieted so she could speak. "I've accepted Imogene's invitation to be an active part of the jamboree again. It's time to let go of the past. Gibson and Mia, Drew and Stacy are our present and future. We should be focused on that. I worry for her. I know you do as well. But I trust Mia to know how to stay safe and who will keep her that way. Imogene tells me Gibson has never brought a female home. Ever. Mia is correct, the boy loves her. I had lasting, real love with Seamus. As you do with Jim, Ellen. Can you imagine your life without him?"

Mia knew her mother had been swayed when she lost the rigidity of her spine with a sigh. Her father kissed her hand as they both looked to her.

"Bring him around more often so we can get to know him. If he's going to be part of the family I should at least know if he likes mashed potatoes or not."

She got back home to find several very large males in her house. There was so much testosterone in the air it took up nearly all the space inside.

They looked up as she entered and she froze at the attention. "Hi." She waved. "Don't worry, I'm not staying. I'm going upstairs to bed."

"Wait, come in, please, Mia." Max stood but it was Gibson who came to her and put his arms around her. "Hi." He nuzzled her neck.

The night was full of unexpected things apparently. It wasn't that he'd never been affectionate to her in the company of others. He was. More by the day as they both became more comfortable with who they were becoming as a couple. But this was work stuff, and he was so focused on that he often forgot about everything else in the room.

He drew her into the living room. "You know Max and my father already, but this is Armando, my youngest brother."

His *little* brother got up and came to her. Towering above her at easily six and a half feet. "It's a pleasure to meet you. Even under the circumstances."

"He's the family's globetrotter so he's been away but once he heard about you he demanded to meet you." Galen kissed her cheek and Gibson coughed and it sounded very much like a growl.

Galen only found that amusing and went back to sit down.

"Out of the way, cretins." Cesar patted the couch next to where he sat. "Come sit with me a moment."

Gibson looked back to his chair on the other side of the room and then to the couch, where there was no more room left. She nearly smiled at his dilemma.

"Give it up. He does this with Renee and Kendra too. You have to deal with it." Max kissed her cheek and then tipped his chin for Gibson to sit down. Which he did. Only on the arm of the couch right next to where Mia had settled in beside Cesar.

"All right, boys. Stop poking at Gibson and tell me what's up."

"We can't be specific, but we'll be away for a while. I don't know how long. But I'm going to ask that you, Kendra and Renee submit to two bodyguards each and that you all stay at the house with Imogene."

"I have a job. I'm supposed to fly Grace to New York tomorrow morning. She's speaking at a conference. I can't let her down."

Cesar patted her hand. "That's fine, *querida*. But you'll have guards with you when you go. They'll escort you to my home when you return. Where it's safest."

She stifled her annoyance. "What do Kendra and Renee think?"

"They're fine with it." Max shrugged.

Galen choked. "Fine is maybe a little misleading. But they're both submitting to this because they know we'll all feel much better with you safe."

"All right. And if any of you get hurt I'm going to be really mad. I sleep with a Glock next to my bed so don't think I'm joking. I will shoot you if you don't make sure Gibson gets back here safely."

Cesar thought this was hilarious.

"As if there was any doubt why she was perfect for me."

She jerked, surprised by Gibson's words. It was the most outward declaration of their relationship he'd made, and she wanted to giggle. Instead she managed to hold it together.

"I'll be right back." Gibson stood. "I'll walk you upstairs."

She waved. "It was nice meeting you, Armando."

"We'll talk soon, Mia. It was my pleasure meeting you."

"When are you leaving?" she asked quietly when they got to the bedroom.

"I'll drive you to National in the morning. You'll be staying in my old room at my parents' house. Robby is your primary guard. I've added Conrad as well. He'll do your driving. I don't know when we'll be back. But I will be. Do you understand?"

"I don't understand much, but I trust you to come back."

"Mia..." He licked his lips. "Thank you for backing me."

"What else could I do? Hm? You need to do this. I know you do. And I know you're strong enough and smart enough to not only come back, but to return victorious. Because you're the Bringer."

"I love you."

She teared up. "Really?"

He snorted. "Have I led you to believe I say things simply to fill up silence?"

"I love you too."

"You're my woman. I'm coming back for you and when I do, we'll talk about imprinting and a bunch of other stuff."

She nodded. "And maybe whatever's gotten into you."

"You have. I can't lie to myself about what you make me feel. It's silly and selfish not to share it with you." He kissed her. "I've got to go back downstairs. I'll be up when we're finished. I'll try not to wake you."

"Puhleeze. If I fall asleep and you don't wake me when we're all alone the night before you hie off on some sort of secret mission, I will kick you in the balls when I wake up."

He winced. "Oh all right. When you put it that way." He kissed her hard and fast. "Be back in a while." And he was gone, leaving her smiling.

"I need you to stay in human form." Gibson spoke to his father, who waved a hand. It was day two of the hunt and time for the next step.

"You don't get to decide that."

"Of course I do. As Bringer this is my hunt."

"This is my jamboree."

"No, it's my jamboree." Max stuffed his clothes into a duffel bag and stashed it in a nearby stand of bushes.

Gibson spoke to his father again. "You're the judge. I need you as a human to keep the rules."

The hunt was ruled by the cat, by the animal the man wore beneath the skin. But this was more than that. They'd already been through the first part of the hunt. Had run this human to ground. This was the next step.

They had some information. The human lawyer's location—though he wasn't a lawyer at all, but one of those fucking human hatemongers pretending to be a lawyer. They'd located him by chance and added what they'd found to the information the wolves had provided when they'd gotten access to a database and had run the pictures in a facial recognition program. Turns out he was on a watch list for hate groups and lived in nearby Framingham.

They'd driven the three-quarters of an hour through spotty traffic and had arrived not too far from the house, which sat up off the road in a quiet neighborhood.

They'd get their revenge, but they needed to find Alberto first. And for that, Cesar needed to remain human so he could call things to a halt before the cats took over and killed the human. They needed the information first.

"Fine. But I will take on the cost. Do you hear me?" He glared at Gibson, who didn't agree.

"This is my job."

"You have done enough killing on behalf of this jamboree. I won't have you bearing it all."

Max looked at his brother, the knowledge of that cost on his features. Gibson knew his brother carried some guilt about what he had to order done in the name of the jamboree. And then he glanced to Cesar, who'd also had to carry that weight when he was Alpha.

"Gibson is the Bringer. It's his role to decide. I will tell you which one of you gets to deliver the killing blow once we get what we need. Now let's go."

Gibson shifted and the cat took over. The night flooded his senses as he breathed in deep. Cats around, yes. And not his cats. *Other* cats.

They crept up the hillside, melting into the shadows, not making a single sound. The cat needed to avenge. Needed to get rid of the threat to its mate. The human up in the house wanted to hurt the mate and that could not be allowed.

The cat wanted to rip and tear and go home to his petite mate. He was not interested in rules or judges.

There were no humans outside and the cat paused to scent the wind. Other cats, but they wore the human skin and were not nearby. Birds. Harsh smells of the machine the humans moved in. The scent that came with the exploding weapons they carried in their hands.

He growled but kept it quiet as the cats all surrounded the house. The human, the father to his human, made a sound, a quick, quiet huff of sound that ordered them all back down the hill they'd crept up.

The cat didn't want to go. The cat wanted to hurt those in the house like they'd hurt his mate. But the call was impossible to ignore, and at last he turned and crept back the way he came, down the hill to where the others had gathered again.

There was speaking and the man shoved up from deep inside. The cat fought him. The man would care about rules the cat had no use for. But in the end, the human pushed hard enough and emerged with a flash of magick and stood.

"There are no guards that I could see. Cats in the house most likely but they're in human form right now. And one human."

"Let's go back up there." Gibson got dressed quickly, strapping his weapons back on. The cat was frustrated it didn't get to hunt but the man was relieved they didn't have to spend days out in the weather looking for their prey. This felt fated. And so he took point, and they headed back up the way his cat had gone. Off the main drive, but it wasn't so steep the man would stumble.

And once they arrived at the house, Cesar simply walked up to the front door and knocked as Max headed around the back and he and Galen to the sides. Armando was in a nearby tree with a sniper rifle should anyone feel the need to run.

"My name is Cesar de La Vega, and I have a grievance with you and yours."

The human who'd opened the door started to close it, but Cesar kicked it open again, knocking the human back to the ground. Max came in through the back and Gibson headed through the window.

And there, in the dining room, cowering under the table, was his cousin.

"Alberto de La Vega, come out and face your accusers." Max thundered this in his best alpha voice. It was so compelling

Gibson felt it in his bones. He turned to see his father with his boot on the throat of the human still on the ground. "Don't move, human. You're very fragile and I'm not ready to break you. Yet."

"Get out before I call the cops!"

Gibson yanked the phone from the wall. "I don't think so, human. I told you back in my office that we don't hold ourselves to human law. You stepped into our world and our law is what counts now."

Max had Alberto by the back of his shirt and tossed him through the doorway, and he ended up in a heap with his human collaborator.

"Search the house. There should be several more. No one leaves." Gibson turned his attention back to his cousin. "Alberto, what do you have to say in your defense?"

Alberto was all bluster, but his fear filled the room. "I have nothing to say to you! Murderer."

"Your father wasn't murdered. He was killed in a challenge. A challenge he called to the death like a fool."

"I claim protection—"

Alberto shut up when Gibson punched him. "You are owed no protection of any kind. You have declared war on de La Vega. You have broken the covenants. Your actions have rendered you outside our laws and as such I am well within my rights to execute you right now."

His father growled before warning Gibson. "Don't you forget, boy. I called it first."

Alberto whined from his place on the floor. "You and your family are a murderous bunch."

"Says the sniveling coward who condemned his entire jamboree to summary execution. It is because we have obeisance to the law that we spared them because they are not responsible for your crimes. But you are responsible for them and you will answer for them."

The human tried to speak again and Cesar pushed harder with his boot. "Your feelings are irrelevant. You hate us enough to help one of our own kill us? You'll be given a real reason to hate and fear us now."

Three more cats were tossed into the living room and then one more.

"Where is your wife?"

"Not here."

Gibson reached down and grabbed the human, his father moving from the way as he stood the human up. "So, David Morris, where is my cousin's wife?"

Gibson gazed into his eyes, letting his cat show. Fear rolled off David in waves.

Alberto risked speaking again. "You want to kill her too?"

"Unlike you, I have no desire to kill my enemy's mate. But neither do I want her freely wandering and plotting to hurt *my* mate." He looked back to the human. "Where is she?"

He blathered an address through his tears.

"Tie him up. We'll take him back for more questioning." He tossed the human to the ground, where his father quickly bound and gagged him. "Galen, call that address in to Dario. Have her picked up and brought to the holding cells. Be careful."

One of the cats Max had brought into the room spoke. "My mom has nothing to do with this! She ran when he told her to. You can't just kill an innocent cat."

"You're one of his sons then? Hm? Yes, you'd be the oldest. I'd like to refer to your words a moment. Mia Porter is an innocent cat and *you* tried to kill her multiple times."

"That's not the same!"

"Why? Because it's someone you care about instead of someone I care about? Mia Porter is *my* someone special. You shot her, shot at her and jumped her on a jogging trail. Like cowards instead of cats. You have no honor. We have laws about protection of our young and our mates. You have violated them." He looked back to his cousin. "As have you. You're coming back with us and we're going to have a long talk. And don't bother looking relieved. You haven't had your death sentence lifted. I'm just postponing it a while until we clear some things up."

He hit his cousin in the temple, knocking him out. "Tie him up. Use the silver-threaded rope. On the others too. Let's get back home."

"I'll call Kendra to let her know to get her spell ready." Max hefted one of the cats he'd knocked out and then tied up. Gibson picked up the human and his father took another. Armando brought the car up and they loaded the prisoners.

He'd have Jack go over every inch of the house. Which was pretty much the only way he'd agreed not to be part of the hunt. The wolves were a powerful ally, as well as being family by that point. But these prisoners were de La Vega business and Gibson would handle exactly how things happened.

He had a plan and he wanted it to play out back at their building.

Chapter Fourteen

It was nearly four in the morning by the time Gibson arrived at his parents' house.

Imogene and the others had set themselves up in the living room, napping on the couches and chairs.

"I'm a fortunate male indeed to be blessed with such a bounty." Cesar looked at them all and then back to Gibson. "Are you sure about this?"

Gibson nodded. "Yes. But I want to tell Mia before the news gets out. She'll be hurt if others know before I get the chance to fill her in."

Max nodded. "Good idea. I've got your back, in any case."

"We'll talk about that too." Galen frowned as they all moved toward the women and each one woke up.

"Why aren't you nestled in bed?" He picked Mia up, and she snuggled into him, wrapping her arms around his neck.

"Waited for you."

"Come upstairs."

"What happened? Is he...gone?"

Gibson shook his head. "No. He's in our custody. As are all the other cats we'd been looking for."

"What now? What aren't you telling me? I can tell when you're not saying everything, you know."

He gave up on getting her upstairs alone and opted for a nearby chair, keeping her in his lap. "I challenged him."

She sat up straighter, all the sleep now gone from her totally clear gaze. "What? Why? Why would do you do that? You don't owe him that. He's nothing. He isn't owed any courtesy of a challenge. Gibson!" She struggled to get free but he held her.

"Wait. Let me explain."

"This had better be damned good, buster, or you're sleeping alone from now on. Offering scum like him a challenge? Why should he get to save face? Why? Huh? He tried to kill you! I know he's related and I'm sorry and all, but I don't care. I don't care about any of them. I care about you. They made their bed. They ran off and then tried to kill you because they are cowards."

Her chin jutted out. She hadn't said they'd tried to kill her. Her anger was that they'd tried to kill him. It only cemented his belief that she was his mate.

The room had gone silent and his mother had that smile of hers. The one she wore when she thought all was right in the world and according to her plans. It was a smile that often scared him. But the female in his lap had claws and she was fully enraged. Which at any other time would have amused him and led to him fucking her senseless right there on the living room carpet. However they were in public and he wanted to explain so she wasn't angry.

"I made the challenge because I want to deal with this treachery openly and honestly. If I'd executed him back at the human's house, it would have been a quietly taken care of problem. I want the whole jamboree to know about this so there is no more sympathy for this creature and his compatriots."

She continued to frown. "You could tell them. They're not stupid. Given the history, what they've done, it's silly to think they'd be resentful."

"My deal is this. I made the challenge publicly. The outcome of the challenge will settle the complaint once and for all. If I lose, the cousins who left will receive amnesty. All but Hal Pepper, but that's done anyway. But if I win, those remaining cousins will be shunned forever. They will be marked for all to see as shunned so there will be no more setting themselves up to be a cancer in anyone else's jamboree. Their line will end as they can't reproduce."

"You can do that?"

"Yes." Kendra spoke from where she sat, giving Gibson a look much like Mia was giving him.

"If they ever set foot in de La Vega territory or in Smithville territory, their lives will be forfeit. Kendra can do a spell which will key in to each of their DNA, and it will alert us to their presence if they decide to be so stupid."

"Their lives are already forfeit! They broke laws. What if the next guy thinks, *hey, why not shoot the Bringer with silver, he won't kill me, he'll give me a chance to kill him instead?*"

Never one to just lay back and take whatever explanation she was fed. Which was a great quality he wished she didn't have right then.

And she wasn't done. "Why not set it to self-destruct? Like on *Get Smart?* They blow up if they show up here again."

His cat pushed close to the surface and hers responded. He held her close.

"I don't like this. At all. I like this zero percent."

"You don't think I can win?"

She punched him in the arm. "I know you'll win. I have no worries about that. But these cats will cheat. We have every reason to believe that so don't even try to argue with me." She glared at Max, who hid a smile and tried to look severe, but totally missed the mark.

"I would never argue any such thing. As it happens I agree with you. I voted that they all be executed on the spot."

Mia narrowed her gaze in Max's direction and then sniffed. "Oh. Well. I like you better." She turned back to Gibson. "You? Not so much right now. However, I'm your second."

Gibson stood, nearly spilling her to the ground. "No you won't be."

She pushed right up into his space and it didn't matter that she was half a foot shorter. "Oh yes I will. I *will* be your second. I *will* be in that challenge ring on the day of the fight and my weapon *will* be hot. I *will* shoot anyone who even thinks about cheating, and I don't care what your feelings on that are."

"You're a mate. You need to stay safe."

"Please do excuse my manners, Imogene," Mia said sweetly and then turned back to Gibson. She poked him in the chest. "You can shove your orders right up your butt. You listen here." She poked him again for emphasis. "I will indeed be your second. I will indeed shoot anyone who cheats. I will break the knees of anyone who tries to stop me. It is my right as your mate—and don't think we're not going to talk about how you just spring that on me without any warning—it's my right as your mate to be your second. I'm invoking that right."

That was a very old law and he looked at his mother suspiciously. Mia hadn't grown up active and well versed in jamboree history. The chances of her knowing that rule seemed very low. But his mother had no guilt on her face over it, and he was confronted by the fact that Mia was right.

He'd publically declared her as his mate and she'd invoked her rights as such.

"This whole thing is to keep you out of danger, damn it. That's not at a challenge ring with a bunch of murderous cats!"

"That's why you should have killed him on the spot." She sniffed and then poked him again. "I was in Iraq for two tours! I was nearly killed by these scumbag human hatemongers. This challenge ring and these gutless cowards don't scare me. At all. You got me? I will be there and that is that. When is the challenge?"

She crossed her arms and each woman in the room got up and moved to stand with her.

He was totally fucked.

"You could have backed me up you know."

Max snorted. "Why? Kendra would have been mad at me. Our mother would have been mad at me, and your sweet Mia would have been mad at me. I don't like it when women are mad at me. I prefer it when they all like me and make me smoothies and turkey sandwiches and have sex with me. The last thing was Kendra specific. If I'd taken your side, Kendra wouldn't be making me sandwiches and she sure wouldn't be having sex with me. Plus, you're stupid. Mia is right. She's got a great eye and she won't be put off by any sympathy toward an old relative. If Alberto cheats, she'll see it and deal with it. And the cats in the jamboree will love it." He shrugged.

"But she'll be in the middle of a challenge ring!"

"Protected by Dario, who will be there with her. No one will hurt her. You know that. She's safer there than any other place

I can imagine. And she's a badass little cat, in case you haven't noticed."

He huffed an annoyed breath. He was so angry at her, angry at the circumstances that he'd put her to bed and gone out for a walk where he'd met Max doing the same thing.

"She loves you, Gibson."

"Ferociously." Gibson nodded. No one had ever loved him that way. Oh sure his parents loved him. But this was different. Mia would give her life for him. Which touched him deeply even as it scared the shit out of him. "I can't live with the idea of her being killed."

"She won't be."

"It'll all be over tomorrow. They underestimate you. Big mistake."

"They were raised by a male who thinks strength comes from how much noise you make." He shrugged. "They don't know about shit. And that's to my favor because Alberto is strong. Just not as strong as me. Or as smart." In fact, they'd found out why the cats had used silver on Gibson that first night but never again, or on Mia. They'd only had enough for that first attack, and they'd run, leaving their ammunition in a hotel room. They'd used regular 9mm ammo from then on, because they hadn't thought ahead to bring enough silver. The ridiculousness of it, the casual nature of plotting to kill a relative aside, only convinced Gibson that his cousin posed no threat at all in the challenge ring.

And just maybe he wanted to publicly beat down anyone who tried to harm his mate.

"But he's a coward. She's right, you can't trust a coward."

"I know. I don't trust him. But I can beat him either way. And if he makes a bad move, I'm under no compulsion not to kill him. He tried to kill my woman, Max. You remember what that feels like."

Max growled and began to pace. "I do. Fuckers. If I could rip them all into pieces I would."

"Exactly. But if anything happens to me, I expect Mia to be taken care of."

Max snorted. "Nothing is going to happen to you. But you know we would. She's ours just as Kendra and Renee are ours."

Mia woke up just a few hours later and snuggled into his body, so warm. She breathed in his scent and gave his side a lick. If he kept her up all night and then dumped this stupid challenge shit on her, she wouldn't feel bad about waking him up.

She nuzzled his neck and he moaned softly as he surfaced from sleep. His hands found her ass and held her tight as she kissed and licked over his neck and shoulders. Her cat was protective; her claws came out a moment, making Mia's mouth water to taste more. To possess this big, strong male in her bed.

His heart beat steady as she listened, her head on his chest.

And then she turned her head and sank her teeth into his biceps.

He snarled, his hand holding her tight, his cock hardening against her belly. "Yes," he hissed.

She held on until she knew the mark would show that day when he was in the challenge ring. Everyone would know he was hers. Most especially the piece of shit who'd tried to kill him multiple times.

Then he pulled her up and rolled on top. "Goddamn." He kissed her so senseless she nearly forgot her own name and when he released her, her lips were swollen and his taste lay against them.

"Just try to get killed now. You're wearing my mark. No one gets to kill you but me."

He grinned as his locks fell around their faces. "I'll keep that in mind."

He slipped inside her and she wrapped her legs around his waist. But it wasn't hard and fast. No it was tortuously slow and deep. His gaze was locked with hers the entire time.

"You're mine, Mia Porter."

She quirked up a grin. "Yes, yes I am. I was hoping you'd figure it out at some point."

"I've known since I opened my eyes to catch you getting naked to shift that very first night."

"And you're mine."

He looked toward the mark on his biceps. "I am indeed."

He continued to stroke into her body, and she was content to be with him, to enjoy the feel of his weight against her body, of the feel of him so thick inside. Time seemed to slow as they were together, no need to speak, tangled in the other.

"You need to come first. Do it for me."

She managed to get a hand between their bodies and found her clit swollen and ready. She was so easy for him it was sort of embarrassing. But she wouldn't have it any other way.

A few strokes, along with the scent of him, the heat of his skin against hers, the little shocks of sensation each time he thrust in and pulled out again, drew her so very close. But when he sank his teeth into her neck, where it met her shoulder, she couldn't hold back. Pleasure rushed through her hard and fast, and there was nothing but Mia and Gibson. They were everything.

He snarled and followed her shortly after, falling to the side and pulling her close until they fell back into sleep for another hour.

Chapter Fifteen

The entire jamboree had crowded inside the gymnasium where the challenge ring had been set up. The air was filled with a macabre excitement as the stands filled with shifters. Several cats she hadn't known very well had approached her to speak. Some to wish Gibson well, some just to say hello and introduce themselves to her.

It would have seemed odd to an outsider, but it was uplifting to be so welcomed, especially at this event. The crowd wanted to see Alberto get his punishment for attempting to harm their own. And Gibson had been right to do it this way, though she'd wait to tell him until after it was all over.

Mia looked for her parents and found them not too far away. She made her way through the crowd to them where her mother hugged her tight.

"Will you sit with us?" Then Ellen's eyes landed on the mark on Mia's neck. Marks were serious enough, but marks given to be seen, deliberately placed on the neck, were declarations of intent. Gibson was telling the entire jamboree that she was his. It tingled as she thought about it, and she looked over her shoulder to where he was speaking quite intently with Max.

Her mother sighed. "All right. I can accept that. Does he make you happy? Really?"

"Yes."

"All right. Grandchildren would be nice, by the way."

She kissed her mother as her father gave her a hug from the side.

"I can't sit with you. I'm his second. I'll be at the edge of the ring."

Her mother's brows flew up. "Young lady, you'll do no such thing."

"If it was Dad down there, what would you do? If you had the skills to protect him, wouldn't you use them?"

Her mother huffed and threw her hands up. "Yes, yes of course. Damn it. Mia, you're going to give me a heart attack. You know that, don't you?"

"I'm safe. I'm not the one in the ring. But if that gutless fool of a cousin of his tries anything, I will take care of it. If he plays by the rules he'll be fine. But he won't. Because you can't turn your back on a gutless man."

Her father nodded.

"I have to go. I need to be there when they recite the rules. Stay up here. No matter what happens, don't rush down there. You're safer up here or out of the building. All right?"

"If you think I'm leaving this building when my baby is in danger, you're out of your head." Her father said this seriously and she squeezed his hands.

"I'll feel better if I know you'll do it. It won't happen, but if it does, I can't be worried about you all at once. Please."

Her father put an arm around her mother's shoulders. "We'll do it."

She heaved a relieved sigh. "Thank you. Thank you really. I love you both. Thank you for being here."

She made her way back down the stands, pausing when she caught sight of Grace and Cade.

Grace hugged her. "Just here to give you moral support. We have no doubt Gibson will be victorious. But I know what it feels like to be in your shoes right now."

She swallowed hard. "Maybe I'm a hopeless fool, but I'm not worried he won't win. I'm just...I hate this and I hate that it's his own blood making him do it."

Grace sighed. "I know that feeling. We're still on for lunch day after tomorrow, right? I'll tell you the story then, and you can tell me about that." She tipped her head to indicate the mark on Mia's neck.

Mia grinned, blushing. "Well." She cleared her throat. "Yes to lunch. I want every detail of the challenge you were in with Cade. I've heard rumors but the truth is always better. I am to understand he was nearly naked." She winked and Grace laughed.

"He was! By the way, did you know that if you shoot a shifter in the kneecaps, it's very hard and very painful to heal? Shattered bone takes a lot of energy to heal. Could take a year or two to fully get back to normal."

She squeezed Grace's hand. "No I didn't know that. Very interesting information. Always good to have that kind. Now keep your eye on that cousin of Gibson's."

And his kneecaps, apparently.

Mia hugged Grace again and turned to head back to the ring.

It was Gibson she watched as she approached where he stood with Dario, Max and the referee, an elder of the jamboree. One of the wolves would serve as a spotter as well. Not Jack as he was too closely allied with Gibson. But Dave, who listened with a serious face.

"This is my second." Gibson held a hand out to her as she approached. The referee looked at her long and hard and then down at the weapon.

"You may not have that in the ring."

"I have no plans to use it unless the opponent cheats. At which time I will invoke the right to use it to prevent the cheating."

"No weapons."

Galen approached. "With all due respect, a second may have a weapon as a means of warning. I can get you the pertinent passages if you'd like, sir." He held up a sheaf of papers. She had the best brothers-in-law ever.

"If you use it unfairly, do know your champion will be disqualified."

"Understood, sir." She averted her eyes, giving him her respect, and he let it go.

He went over the rules. First man to hit the ground of the ring for longer than twenty-five seconds would forfeit, and the deal they'd brokered would go into effect. She hated this part. In her opinion, Alberto should go to prison at the very least. But it wasn't for her to decide.

The referee told them to get into positions and moved to go give the rules to the other challenger.

Gibson took her aside. "I love you. Be careful. Dario will be right next to you. If anything happens, let him take over. He knows what to do." Gibson smiled when he saw the mark on her neck again. She'd worn a shirt with a wide neck so it would be easily identifiable. "I like that."

She grinned. Tiptoeing up to kiss him. "Me too. I've got your back."

He took her hands. "I know. It's a miracle to me."

And then he took his shirt off and moved to stand in his spot. She heard the whispers about the marks. Heard the disappointment of a few females. Tough luck! He was hers and she wasn't giving him back, sharing him or letting anyone kill him either.

Alberto came out wearing a sneer. Stupid move given his already tenuous situation. The crowd, which had been curious, was repulsed, and the hum of conversation went in a negative direction. She rolled her eyes.

Tension in the room made her cat nervous and focused on Gibson. The scent of sweat and fear only made things worse. Her cat wanted to jump on Alberto's back, beat him to shreds and grab Gibson and get out of there.

The woman knew better, though it was easier not to kill anyone because she knew she could shoot Alberto when he cheated.

The referee made the call and the challenge opened.

Gibson stepped in and delivered the first blow. So hard it knocked Alberto off his feet and to the floor. Sadly he got up after five seconds, brushing himself off. He circled but Gibson eluded all his attempted strikes, landing several more of his own.

Gibson had so much focus it was impossible not to be impressed. Mia watched him, knew he didn't miss a single thing about how Alberto moved and attempted to strike.

She shifted her attention back to Alberto. He might have had the blood of leadership in his veins, but he'd grown soft. He was slower than Gibson. Like by a mile. Gibson's movements were fluid and graceful. A man who spent time training. Alberto was a big cat, but he wasn't hard.

Alberto shifted and leapt at Gibson, who'd already shifted and slammed Alberto down to the mat, his cat snarling.

Alberto's cat had a long set of scratches down its side where Gibson had caught him. He tried to shift back but it was slow. Gibson was already there and punched him in the face and then the side.

Alberto was outmatched on every single level. He wasn't faster. He wasn't harder. He wasn't stronger or smarter. Mia saw the exact moment when this realization came over Alberto's face. He'd only landed two blows to Gibson's dozens. He stumbled but kept his feet. And then he dipped and grabbed something his second had thrown him.

Her weapon was out of the holster, and she'd thumbed the safety off before he'd even straightened.

"I call a cheat!" She projected her voice loudly, knowing both Alberto and the referee had heard.

But Alberto didn't stop, he made to lunge at Gibson so she shot the ground once at Alberto's feet.

"I said, I call a cheat. Hold!"

It all seemed to happen in slow motion as Alberto turned with a full-throated roar and lunged toward her, clearing the ring.

She planted her feet and kept her cool, squeezing the trigger once, twice, three times. Alberto hit the ground.

"Don't kill him!" Dario shouted over the ringing of her ears.

She wanted to so very badly, but she obeyed as the crowd all around them went wild, screaming and shouting.

"She's broken the law. This challenge is forfeit!" Alberto choked from his place on the ground. Blood oozed from where she'd shattered each kneecap.

"You have attempted to cheat in the full view of the panel and the referee. You were told to cease by the second, who fired a shot into the ground, not at you. You not only refused to stop, but you broke the ring and attacked a second along with the spectators directly behind her. You have broken our laws, Alberto de La Vega. The forfeit is yours."

Dario hauled Alberto to his feet. "You'll heal. Consider yourself lucky she didn't aim for your head. Now you and yours have some ground to make. Remember de La Vega territory stretches several hundred miles in all directions. You have two hours, and this time, we'll know if you come back."

"So what? What do I care about a spell?"

"You'll care because the spell is now keyed to your DNA. If you step foot into de La Vega territory again your heart will explode." Kendra said it in a low voice, laced with menace. "Stay off my land or your life will be over. And anyone else associated with you."

"You wouldn't!"

Kendra smiled. "Oh I would. You see, I have a pretty big hate-on for you and yours and all those who attack us for being different. You not only tried to harm my cats, but you consorted with those humans who seek to do all Others in. I am Alpha of the de La Vega jamboree and you are beneath contempt. So just try it. Come back and see if I'm lying, and you'll no longer be a problem at all."

White faced, he allowed his sons to take him away.

"I'm on it." Dario spoke to Gibson, who simply pulled Mia into his arms.

"You saved my life yet again. Clearly I need to keep you around just for that."

She hugged him tight. "I wanted to kill him. Dario wouldn't let me."

"My lovely Mia, covered in blood, gun in your hand, death threats on your lips. My perfect female." He stepped back and the crowd hushed as he addressed them. "It is my sincere hope that this chapter of our history is done. Alberto and his compatriots are banned from our lands and from the lands of his other jamboree. We will fight to the death to protect our cats and our land. I will continue to do so with this female at my side. And I hope to do it with her not only as my mate, but as my wife."

Her hands shook from the adrenaline still in her system, and she used the back of her hand to wipe the blood from her face. Her father appeared and handed her a handkerchief.

"What do you say, Mia? Will you be mine for the rest of our lives? Have my babies? Keep me in line and out of trouble?"

Her voice shook as much as her hands did. "I-I'm not sure even I have the power to keep you out of trouble, Gibson. But I'll marry you and give it my best shot."

He fell to his knees and she went with him, hugging him because he was real and all right and all hers. Relief rushed through her, bringing tears to her eyes.

"Shhh, don't cry. It's over now."

"They're relief tears. It's the adrenaline," she lied. "I love you." And that was the truth.

"Me too, you crazy female. Glad you didn't kill him. I was worried for a moment."

"I wanted to. Really badly. But I figured we needed to have the referee make the ruling while he was alive. Those kneecaps will be hard to grow back. Learned something new today. Shattered bone can't be reknit like a slash in his skin. It'll be painful. And he'll probably feel it for a few years. I hope he thinks of me every time he gets a twinge."

He grinned, kissing her soundly. "You're so hot when you're vicious. Come on." He hauled her to her feet. "A shower and then an engagement dinner is in order. Followed by rigorous sex once we're alone." He whispered the last part.

"Rigorous? Will there be a test?"

He laughed. "You make me laugh. I love that about you. I'm happy to test you."

"Only if there's discipline if I don't get it right."

"You're playing with fire, missy."

She laughed, taking his hand. "Come on then my beautiful handful of a mate. Let's wash off the blood and celebrate our victory and our engagement."

"You got it." He held her hand and drew her through the crowd of well-wishers and out the back door.

About the Author

To learn more about Lauren Dane, please visit www.laurendane.com. Send an email to Lauren at laurendane@laurendane.com or stop by her message board to join in the fun with other readers as well. http://www.laurendane.com/messageboard.

He has the one thing she never thought she deserved.
A place to belong...

Revelation
© 2010 Lauren Dane
de La Vega Cats, Book 2

At long last, Kendra Kellogg has found her sister—but she's no closer to filling the gaps in her past. The magick that brought them together makes them targets for dark mages intent on finishing what started with their mother's murder.

As if her life wasn't chaotic enough, in barrels the one thing she doesn't expect, Max de La Vega. He's six-and-a-half-feet of cocoa-brown alpha male. He's strong, intelligent, sexy and intense. Everything she'd wanted in a man. And he scares the hell out of her. Still healing from a disastrous past relationship, she wonders if she'll ever have that kind of forever.

The next in line to run his jaguar jamboree, Max is unused to hearing "no". Once he knows what he wants, he assumes he'll get it. And he wants Kendra. She deserves happiness and it's his mission to give it to her.

When dark mages attempt to steal her magickal energy, Max's cat agrees with the man—Kendra is his to protect and he will stop at nothing to keep her safe. She can push him away as hard as she likes, he's not going anywhere.

Warning: Prickly, grumpy witch, bossy alpha male, scorching hot sexual attraction, toss in some bad words, a little bit of violence and a whole lot of action.

Available now in ebook and print from Samhain Publishing.

He can't fight his inner beast, but she can tame it.

Hunter's Prey
© *2012 Moira Rogers*
Bloodhounds, Book 2

Ophelia retired from life as a prostitute, but her new position is even more complicated. Managing the bloodhound manor in Iron Creek is difficult and time-consuming, a job she enjoys less with each passing day. Then there's her inconvenient attraction to Hunter. The newly turned hound seems eager to enjoy her company, but wary of anything more intimate.

Having survived the violence of his first full moon out of a cage, Hunter isn't looking forward to his first new moon. Ophelia offers to be the woman who sates his needs during the three long days of sexual fury, but he can't abide the thought of hurting her in a state of mindless lust. Especially since she longs to settle into a respectable life, and his needs are anything but respectable.

Their mutual goal is simple: avoid entanglements. It's a solid plan, at least until a vampire drug lord and a couple of nosy Guild representatives force them to work together to defend their friends and everything they hold dear—including each other.

Warning: Contains a mostly feral, vampire-hunting hero and a tough survivor of a heroine whose retired-hooker heart is more steel than gold. Also included: dangerous frontier intrigue, fancy brothels, mad-scientist weapons and a good dose of wicked loving in an alternate Wild West.

Available now in ebook from Samhain Publishing.

www.samhainpublishing.com

Green for the planet.
Great for your wallet.

PUBLISHING

It's all about the story...

Romance

HORROR

Retro ROMANCE

www.samhainpublishing.com

CPSIA information can be obtained at www.ICGtesting.com
Printed in the USA
LVOW062052280613

340753LV00002B/82/P